SNOWBLIND

Leigh Jarrett

Published by Steambath Press (self-published)
An LJ Gay Romance

Paperback published March 2023
ISBN-13: 978-1-998008-00-1

Chapter One | James

It was either going to be the death of him or it was going to breathe exhilaration into his bones. Either way, it was going to be epic. James dismounted the *Cliff Chair* and headed for the double-black diamond run that had been calling his name since before he crawled out of bed.

Snow had a way of doing that—summoning him. Since James had been old enough to walk, every winter without fail, he'd had a pair of skis strapped to his feet. His family was big into mountain sports. Skiing, snowboarding, and bombing around on snow machines in the winter. Mountain biking and hiking during the seasons when there was no snow. This weekend was on the cusp of the conflicting seasons. Early spring. Blankets of snow—and bright sunshine.

Perfection.

James lowered his goggles from his helmet onto his eyes. The world around him turned orange. The sun was bright; the snow sparkling. Without goggles, you ran the risk of becoming snowblind. He clipped his back foot onto his snowboard and glided toward the cliff edge.

There weren't a lot of people hitting this run today. Normally, his two brothers would be right there beside him, but James had decided to take this trip alone. Even though he had been living on his own for years, James' family habitually joined him for most of his competitions and free weekends. James was a professional snowboarder; away competing for much of the winter and spring. His family would usually share a chalet with him if they tagged along.

Not this weekend, though. This weekend was for himself. Some time on his own. Rest and relaxation away from the marital expectations and religious rhetoric his family was forever placing upon him. He needed time to think. Snowboard, think, and get his mind back in the game.

James tightened the straps on his gloves and edged toward the slope, shuffling forward across the snow. He tried to clear his mind; it had been in turmoil all week. After three years of slogging through a relationship, his fiancé, Julie, had finally called it quits. Words like *absent* and *distant* hurled at him across the room had brought their time together to an end.

She had walked out on him.

One year ago, it seemed like the right thing to do: ask Julie to marry him. He met her in college, and they had hit it off. But it soon became evident, in James' mind, that they made better friends than life partners. If only he had been brave enough to share that with *her*.

He had allowed himself to be controlled, swept along with his family's expectations. There had been pressure from home about it being time to settle down and start a family; both things James wanted to do—just not with Julie. The truth was, he *had* been absent from their relationship. Going through the motions, day after day, imagining what it would be like to be in love with the person you were about to marry. It had beat him down, the lying, and the apathy he felt.

Julie had finally had enough.

He had broken her heart. Something he was not proud of. He had deliberately pulled away until Julie took the hint. He had taken the coward's way out.

Now it plagued him; whether he would ever find true love after the mess he had made of Julie's life. Everyone in church likely knew he caused the breakup. That he had treated her unfairly. Women would not be lining up to take their chance with him. But then, maybe he didn't deserve to form an intimate, loving connection with someone. It seemed unattainable.

Falling in love—it was a dream.

One that needed to be filed away.

James exhaled as he examined the steep drop of the *Parachute Bowl*. He needed to focus on the *intimate connection* between his board and the snow. This was a love he knew well. His love for the sport was the only love he felt comfortable with. He leaped off the crest and sped down the bowl, the swooshing and crunching of the snow beneath his board making his heart sing.

He was at home here. Among the snow-laden trees. A path laid out before him, cutting back and forth, riding the immense expanse of snow as he made his way down the mountain. The cool air streamed in through his nose. His heart hammered in his chest; his arms outstretched.

He was soaring.

James angled his board, concentrating on keeping his footing. He could handle this. He could handle anything the mountain threw at him. Shivers ran up his spine, his breath quickening.

This was pure freedom. On the runs, alone. Away from the crowds of competitions. Competing brought him a different kind of high. His events were Freestyle: Halfpipe and Big Air. Performing tricks, achieving incredible heights, and pursuing a *Wow Factor* to impress the judges. Racing down a mountainside, testing his skills on different terrains, and completing a run intact; pleasure radiated to his very soul. But this, times like today … this was special.

He reached the bottom and coasted down the *Woodpecker* to the lift. The line was long for the *Blackforest Express,* but he needed to give his legs a rest on an easier run. He would hit a blue run next. Another three or four runs would be all he could fit in before the mountain opened for night skiing. He had no interest in the runs on offer at night. Sure, the lit pathways were fun, but there was no challenge in the decline and there were far too many people for his liking.

He shuffled along, obediently, working his way to the front of the line. To the top then down another run. And another. The rest of the afternoon streaked by.

Standing in line for his last run of the day, James was surprised when someone slid into him, nearly knocking him off his feet, a spray of wet snow fanning up into his face. He cleared the snow from his cheeks, looking around to see who the asshole was.

"What the hell?"

"Sorry … wasn't paying attention."

James peered at the face beaming at him; intense baby blue eyes, crazy long lashes, brown, curly hair erupting from beneath a florescent green helmet. He knew that face well. He had been competing against Corey Taylor since he started his professional snowboarding career at age thirteen. They had never spent much time getting to know each other.

Much meaning little to none. They were competitors after all.

He was convinced Corey had slid into him on purpose. Trying to annoy him. James wasn't going to play that game. He was going to remain civil. He looked over his shoulder. The lineup behind them was grumbling about Corey *cutting in.* Just right. This was Corey's home mountain. He should know better than to tick off potential fans and admirers.

He turned his attention back to Corey. There was a serious rivalry happening between them. Truly. They were fierce competitors. But it was going to be difficult to stay mad at Corey.

The playful glint in the guy's eyes was infectious.

Chapter Two | Corey

What were the chances? James freakin' Cartwright. Corey shook his head in disbelief as James approached the lineup for the *Blackfoot Express* lift. This wasn't James' home mountain. James was from Vancouver Island. A product of Mount Washington. And whereas Corey tended to visit Calgary for off-season training, James headed to Quebec. James had family there. The chances of them running into each other on their off times was remote, but a couple of times during the day, Corey had thought he spotted James. Now it was confirmed.

His *crush,* James, was snowboarding his home mountain in Kelowna—*Big White.*

Corey slammed into James, his heart rabbiting away in his chest. He was expecting a scowl to be shot at him when James saw who it was. The look he received from James was decidedly pleasant. It warmed him through—James' gentle brown eyes watching him; his full lips poised before he spoke. Corey wasn't sure what, if anything, they might have to say to each other. Their few interactions over the years had always been light-hearted—friendly. But had been limited to "Nice run", "Epic bail", "Congratulations" and the like.

This free-time, chance meeting scenario was unknown territory.

Not that it would lead to anything. It was the story of his life … falling for the wrong guys. Either they were emotionally unavailable, straight, or not interested in settling down. James fit neatly into the second category. James' girlfriend was a common fixture at competitions. She and James' family. Plus, there were rumors they were right-wing, ultra-Christian types. Not exactly gay-friendly. Still, that didn't stop Corey from crushing on James. His toned body, shaggy blond hair, and a smile that could light up a thousand galaxies spoke to his heart.

Corey was going to press on … and talk to James now that he had got his attention.

"What are you doing all the way out here in the interior?" Corey asked.

"I needed a break." James smiled. "And I love the snow here."

"It's a gorgeous day to be out in it."

"Sure is."

"You on your last run?"

James nodded and adjusted the goggles on his helmet.

"Mind if I join you?" Corey asked.

"Ah …" James appeared to hesitate, then tipped his head to one side. "Sure."

Corey released an exhalation of relief, then sucked in a breath of uncertainty. His toes were tingling at the prospect of hanging with James. Even if it was only for one run. Even if he didn't have a chance with him. It would be the most time he had ever spent near the guy. By all accounts, James was amenable. Friendly, outgoing—and one hell of a great snowboarder.

He wanted to know more.

If nothing else than to torture himself.

The lineup advanced toward the lift. They slid along in silence. It wasn't until they were hoisted onto a lift chair that James spoke.

"How many runs have you done today?" he asked.

"Five or six. Legs are turning a bit rubbery." Corey glanced at James. There was that smile of his … and in response to something Corey had said. His gut clenched, fluttering. "This will be my last run as well. I don't go in for the night skiing."

"Yeah … me either."

Corey leaned forward in the chair, watching the people below on the green run. He pointed at something and laughed. "Do you see that kid? Can't be more than four years old."

James peered down at the snow below them. "That was me as a kid. Every weekend with the family. As soon as I could walk, my parents put a pair of skis on me. Hauled me around on the flat snow at the end of their poles. By the time I was three, I was killing the beginner run." James grinned. "Mastered the snowplow anyway."

"No wonder you're so good."

James inhaled a deep breath. "I love being out here." He turned to face Corey. "What about you? When did you start cutting up the slopes?"

"I was a bit older. My parents enrolled me in an after-school snowboarding program when I was in grade three. Took to it right away. I was spotted by a sponsor when I was fourteen. Things got pretty serious after that. My parents are perfectionists. I had to be the best."

"We've certainly battled it out more than a few times."

Corey chuckled. "You've presented me with a challenge, that's for sure."

"Yeah … hey, congratulations on the Half Pipe win in the Freestyle Nationals by the way."

"Thanks." Corey nodded. "Congrats on the Big Air win." He leaned back in the ski lift chair, his shoulder packed in against James', their thighs touching despite the fact they were in a four-person chair. Corey had made a point of sitting close.

The sensation was electric. To keep his body from responding, he concentrated on the weather. It was changing. The sun had disappeared, replaced by a white sky. It was about to start snowing.

"Looks like snow," James said as he shifted in his seat. The chair swayed in response. Corey gripped the safety bar. Their proximity was making James uncomfortable.

"And fog if it doesn't." Corey laughed. "They don't call it Big White for nothing."

"True." James looked around, seemingly at the scenery. "You headed to the Winter Games next week?"

"Wouldn't miss it … you?"

"I might give it a miss this year."

"You not interested in the Olympics team picking you up?"

James exhaled. "I'd love that, but I don't know that I'm good enough."

"Pfft." Corey shoved James in the shoulder. "Of course, you are."

James smiled. "Thanks." He looked down at his gloves, adjusting them as they approached the top of the lift. They both shifted forward on the chair in preparation for dismounting.

When they finally reached the top, Corey abandoned any hopes he had of snagging James' romantic attention. The guy was straighter than a brand-new cross-country ski pole.

That didn't mean he couldn't have fun with him.

"You want to head to *Telus Park*?" Corey asked as he pulled away down the ramp to the lift. "Have a bit of fun?"

"Sounds like a good end to the day."

James followed Corey as he boarded down *Easter Chutes* to *Sundance*, landing them at the top of the terrain snowboard and ski park filled with jibs, jumps, halfpipes, and snow cross courses. James took off down the slope toward the halfpipe area. Corey joined him. It was nice not to be competing against James. They were just going to have some fun. After about an hour in the park, they found themselves hesitating at the bottom near the lift. The overhead lights had flicked on.

"Have you had enough?" Corey asked.

"I'm exhausted … and I'm hungry."

"I hear you." Corey headed toward *Easy Street*, James at his side. When James veered toward him, shoved him, and took off down the wide, easy slope, a huge grin spread across Corey's face. The game was on. He went after James, streaking up behind him. James caught him off guard, slowing and grabbing Corey's coat. They ended up tumbling into a snowbank together.

Tumbling, laughing—with snowboards releasing their hold. It was irresponsible. He wasn't sure what had gotten into James to initiate the game. They finished rolling.

James landed on top of him.

The weight, the pressure of James' body …

Corey's heart thundered in his chest.

For a moment, he imagined James was considering kissing him. He hovered above Corey, looking down at him. Corey's mind ran amok with the possibility. Then James scrambled off him. Corey's steamy daydream deflated at the ridiculousness of where his mind had gone.

It was just like him, seeing attraction where there wasn't any. Regardless, it was a great end to the day, but Corey didn't want it to end there.

There was one more thing he wanted to do with James today.

Chapter Three | James

James cruised into the village beside Corey. The snow was coming down hard in massive white flakes that were blanketing the square. They'd had some good runs—full of awesome snowboarding antics. It had brought some much-needed levity to James' trip.

After cruising and jumping in *Telus Park*, they had made a game of trying to catch one another—knock each other over. A collision had landed them both in a snowbank. They were lucky they hadn't broken anything. That would have been career-crushing. It had been utterly irresponsible, but he had felt the need to jostle with Corey a bit before their day came to an end.

He smiled. He hadn't had that much fun in a long time. His life was all about training. A chance to hit the slopes and just enjoy his board was a rarity. He looked at Corey. James was glad he had run into Corey—or Corey had run into him. The guy was a riot—fun and energetic.

"So … dinner," Corey said.

"Yeah, I'm going to head in and start cooking."

"You stayin' on the mountain?"

"Yeah."

"Any chance I can entice you into eating out with me?"

James shook his head. "Nah. To be honest, I need a nap before I even contemplate dinner."

Corey visibly sighed. It almost made James change his mind. Corey was obviously disappointed by his answer. But

James was sticking to it. He was tired.

"How about later?" Corey asked. He pointed in the direction of Snowplow Pete's. "We could meet up tonight. Have a couple of drinks. Listen to some live music."

James scowled. He had noticed earlier that the perimeter of Snowplow Pete's was decorated with rainbow flags. The kind the gays used to mark their territory. He had overheard people talking in the lift lineups about a *Winter Pride* celebration happening. What they had to be proud of, he wasn't sure. He had never known a gay person. The whole gay lifestyle wasn't on his radar.

"Sure. If we go somewhere else," James answered.

Corey crossed his arms. "What's wrong with Pete's?"

"They have all that gay stuff going on tonight."

"And ..."

"And I don't want to hang out with them."

Now it was Corey's turn to scowl. The action caused his brilliant blue eyes to partially disappear behind his lids. "Have you got something against gay people?"

"No ... no ... not really." James sighed. He hadn't meant to upset Corey. "I don't know. I've never hung around with gay people before."

Corey laughed. "Oh, I am *positive* you have."

"No, really. I haven't."

Corey took a step toward James and lay a hand on his shoulder. "Buddy, you have been hanging out with one for the past hour."

James jerked away. "You're gay?"

"Not officially." Corey shrugged. "Only my close friends and family know."

"Then why are you telling me?"

"I thought we were having a good time together. Becoming

friends."

"We *were*."

James looked toward the building he was staying in. The conversation was making him uneasy. He wanted to head back to his suite, have a nap, and make dinner. Not have to struggle with the realization that the guy he had been having so much fun with was gay.

He peered back at Corey. The look on Corey's face was one of distress, his pink lips close to pouting, his thick eyelashes fluttering up and down on his cheeks. He looked like a puppy that had been accused of doing something wrong. James sighed. Maybe it wouldn't be so bad. He would be with Corey, a guy he had enjoyed hanging with.

What's the worst that could happen?

"You're set on going to Pete's?" he asked.

"It's why I came up this weekend … *Winter Pride*."

"Will you know anyone there?"

Corey shrugged. "Probably. Tommy D'Angelo is playing. I've seen him quite a few times during pride events in Kelowna. He has a following. I'll likely know someone."

"Will we be hanging out with them?"

"Not if you don't want to."

"All right." James nodded. "I'll go but I am not playing your wingman or anything." He unfastened his boot from the board, lifted it, and placed it under his arm.

"Deal." Corey pointed toward the gondola. "Okay. I'm off to my car to get changed."

"You not staying here tonight?"

"Nah. I'll stick around for a bit then drive home. No point in wasting money on a place when I have an apartment back in town. I'm just down in Black Mountain. It's not far."

James tightened his grip on his board. He was disappointed

to hear Corey wasn't sticking around. In the few minutes they had been standing there talking, James had imagined snowboarding with Corey again tomorrow. Maybe Corey would drive back if he asked.

"Okay, well ... I'll see around what ...," James said. "Eight?"

Corey started sliding toward the gondola. "Eight. I'll meet you inside." He grinned and slid away. Corey knew damn well it would take a lot for him to walk into that pub tonight on his own. Before James could object to the idea, Corey was halfway across the concourse.

James stood and watched Corey as he became obscured by the falling snow, his fluorescent helmet bobbing along as he made his way to the gondola that would take him to the parking lot.

He sighed. The air seemed empty without Corey filling it. It was an odd sensation. James turned for the condo complex he was staying in and trudged through the snow toward it. Within moments he was inside in the warmth. He stripped off his snowboarding gear and flicked on the gas fireplace. The warm glow from the flames filled the room.

James plopped down on the sofa, then stretched out on it. He hauled a blanket onto his body, making sure to cover his feet and shoulders. He was chilled. He closed his eyes and sleep descended on him. The last thing he remembered seeing in his mind was Corey's face.

He awoke with a start and scrambled for his phone. He wasn't sure how long he had been asleep. He breathed a sigh of relief when he saw it was only six-thirty. He still had an hour and a half until he was meeting with Corey. It gave him time to make dinner and clean himself up.

Before coming up the mountain, James had stopped at the

grocery store to stock up on supplies. Spending all day on the mountain required a lot of calories. He might have overdone it but the last thing he wanted was to be hungry. It was always an option to go out for dinner, but James loved cooking. He particularly liked sitting at home in front of a warm fire eating dinner. He dug cans of tomato sauce out of a bag, removed some ground beef, onions, green peppers, and mushrooms from the fridge, and retrieved the pasta from the far end of the counter.

He started with the mushrooms, sautéing them in a bit of olive oil, then added some chopped onion. There were a few other things he needed. James peered into the grocery bag and pulled out some garlic, a jar of instant coffee, and some Italian spice. The condo would have sugar in the cabinets. The garlic and green peppers went in next, then the ground beef. After that was browned, he added a cup of water, a teaspoon of instant coffee, and a pinch of sugar.

James grabbed himself a beer from the fridge as that simmered, then set some water to boiling in a pot. He opened the cans of tomato sauce and added them to the ground beef mixture along with the spices. That set to a low bubble, he sat back on the sofa and stared into the flames.

His mind turned to Corey again. There was something about Corey that made James want to spend more time with him. Corey's laughter and exuberance for life were contagious. He was having trouble reconciling that with the fact the guy was gay. He couldn't see it. James had seen gay guys on television, marching in their parades. Corey wasn't anything like them.

The sound of the water boiling broke him from his thoughts. He rose to his feet, headed to the kitchen, and dumped a huge handful of spaghetti noodles into the water. He retrieved a container of parmesan cheese from a second grocery bag. He shook it up to make sure it wasn't clumped together. It wasn't long until the noodles were done.

After locating the biggest plate he could find, he piled a mountain of food onto it, gathered up his utensils, and headed back to the fire. There was no coffee table, so he had to make do with his lap. It was risky, but he was stripped down to his thermal underwear. He wasn't worried about spilling sauce on his clothes. He twirled the noodles and took a mouthful.

Amazing.

As James chewed, Corey popped into his mind again. He wondered if he should have invited Corey to have dinner with him. It was good, and it would have been the polite thing to do, but he had badly needed that nap. Entertaining someone wouldn't have allowed him that.

James turned on the television. The clock above it showed that the time was seven-thirty. He needed to get ready soon if he was going to arrive on time. He finished his plate, took it to the kitchen, and set it in the sink. He would worry about dishes later. After packaging up the remainder of the sauce, he headed to the bathroom for a shower.

The hot water felt great, soothing his aching muscles. He might have pushed himself too hard today. He grinned. When he and Corey had plowed into that snowbank, they had ended up in a tangle of arms, legs, and snowboards. It had taken some doing to extract themselves from the pile they had created. James' stomach fluttered at the memory. On the chair lift, they had been close to one another—touching. It had made him uncomfortable—the closeness. But in the snowbank, he had landed fully on top of Corey. It had taken him a moment to react. He remembered looking down into Corey's eyes, pondering them, before he righted himself.

James shook his head. Corey's eyes reminded him of pools of tranquil, blue water. Glittering up top, but so much depth behind them. He stepped out of the shower and dried himself off. It was going to be jeans and a thick, cream cable-knit sweater. It was one of the few extra pieces of clothing he had packed.

He looked at himself in the mirror. He was nothing special in his eyes. His brothers had more going for them in the looks department. He ran his hand through his blond hair as he examined his face. He wasn't going to bother shaving. The dark stubble gave him a rugged look he liked. He touched the ring in his nose and grinned at himself in the mirror. His parents had freaked out when they first spotted it. It was the only act of rebellion he had ever pulled.

He looked at his phone. It was eight o'clock. Time to head out. He pulled on his ski jacket and his battered and worn snow boots. Again … not much choice in clothing, but it wasn't like he was trying to impress anyone. He was meeting with a buddy for a drink. That's it.

The walk to Snowplow Pete's only took him a few minutes. The snow was picking up in intensity along with the wind. The rainbow flags were whipping about in the gusts of air. Colors flying. Letting everyone know what was happening. His heart leaped in his chest, and he almost changed his mind. He wasn't sure what to expect if he went inside. His upbringing clawed at his insides. This was enemy territory—wasn't it?

James approached the outer doors but didn't go in. He stood in the cold, looking through the small windows. The place was packed. He looked at his phone. It was quarter past eight. Corey would be waiting for him, wondering if he was going to show up.

He pulled his hands out of his pockets and placed one on

the door. He still hadn't asked Corey if he wanted to meet up again the next day to go snowboarding—and they hadn't exchanged numbers. That was going to be his excuse. He pulled the door open. The lively roar of the crowd intensified. He steadied his breathing and pressed forward, angling his way through a multitude of bodies, his eyes searching for the one face that would calm his nerves. James spotted Corey, sitting alone at a bar table at the same moment as Corey caught sight of him.

Corey's smile was electric, like a beacon. James felt himself relaxing as he moved toward him. Standing in front of him, Corey pounded his shoulder in welcome.

"I didn't think you were coming," Corey shouted above the din.

"I almost didn't." James removed his jacket, covered one of the stools with it, then took a seat. He hadn't thought he was going to admit that to Corey, but it felt like he should.

"There's nothing to be worried about." Corey moved away from his seat. "Can I get you a beer?" He grinned. "Unless you're afraid of sitting here on your own."

James ducked his gaze away from Corey's watchful eyes. "I can manage."

"Excellent … pint of IPA?"

"That's good, yeah."

As Corey stood at the bar, James kept an eye on him. Corey looked different in street clothes. His shoulders and thighs were muscular but lean, his hips narrow. Corey was wearing a long-sleeved, red t-shirt. It fit tight to his body, showing off his biceps.

James looked out at the crowd as Corey approached their table.

Corey was smirking.

"Like what you see?" Corey sat across the table from James. "Caught you watching me."

James' face flushed red. He hadn't realized he had been staring. He had been fascinated by the differences in Corey when he was wearing something other than snowboarding gear.

"You look different."

"Like good different … or bad different?"

James furrowed his brow. The question flustered him. There was no right answer. He took a sip of his beer. Corey was studying him, waiting for an answer, but appeared to give up, and shrugged his shoulders. Corey took a long swallow from his pint glass and perused the room.

"I'm not seeing too many people I know," Corey said. "A few … but not many."

"Other gays?"

Corey turned in his seat, leaned on the table facing James, and narrowed his eyes at him. "You say *gays* like it's a bad word."

"I didn't mean it to sound that way." James spun his glass on the coaster. "I am so far out of my depth here." He chanced a glance into Corey's eyes. "I didn't mean to hurt your feelings."

Corey exhaled. "My feelings are fine. They're a lot tougher than most. It's you I worry about. Exactly how sheltered was your upbringing?"

"I'll tell you another time."

Corey winked at him. "So, there's going to be another time."

James rolled his eyes and smiled. Corey was flirting with him. All in good fun, of course, but it was a side of Corey he hadn't expected to see. In no way did Corey fit into his preconceived notions about what the gay community looked like. He glanced around the room. Some of the people, it was obvious they bent that way. Others … it was anyone's guess.

"What should I say instead of *gays*?"

"The 2SLGBT2Q+ community would be nice."

James huffed out a laugh. "That's a bit of a mouthful."

"That's what *he* said."

It took a second for the innuendo to sink in. James' cheeks prickled with embarrassment. He buried his face in his drink as someone walked onto the stage area. It was a tall woman dressed in a tight, shimmery black bodysuit. The pant portion appeared to be ass-less. This was exactly what James had been concerned about. Getting an eyeful of something he wasn't prepared for.

She raised the microphone to her lips.

"Good evening, bitches. For those that don't know me, and fuck you if you don't, I'm Trixie Lamour and we have a great show for you tonight."

The swearing caught him off guard. That and the risqué outfit had James reconsidering his decision to join Corey. His mom would be horrified if she found out he had been here for this.

His curiosity won out.

James stared at Trixie. She was gorgeous but something wasn't right. The low register of her voice … it wasn't computing. He studied her as she walked back and forth across the stage, a steady stream of obscenities, sexual innuendos, and cutting observations of the audience filling the room. James squirmed in his chair; his beer gripped tight in his palm as he watched her.

"What's wrong?" Corey leaned toward him. "You look confused."

James dipped his eyebrows as he looked at Corey. "Is that a guy?"

Sure, he had heard of drag queens. Who hadn't? But James had never seen one in person. They were one of the abominations his mother and her group of women went on about. How they shouldn't be allowed near children. Her group had protested outside libraries during *Drag Story Time* numerous times, calling drag queens pedophiles, and insisting they were grooming the children. It had been pointless. The children's activity was incredibly popular.

Corey smiled. "Yeah, it's a guy."

James perused Trixie's body.

"I can see where you're looking," Corey said. "It's still there. Just tucked away."

James shivered but couldn't take his eyes off Trixie. Aside from the language, he seemed harmless enough. After an introduction from Trixie, a musician stepped onto the stage area.

"Wait until you hear this guy," Corey shouted across the table. Tommy D'Angelo warmed up his fingers on the keyboard and the crowd hushed as he adjusted his microphone.

"Welcome to *Winter Pride*!" Tommy's voice was clear and loud, echoing throughout the room. He played a few chords for effect. James sat up straighter. If Corey was excited by the prospect of this guy playing music, he was going to pay attention. Tommy's outfit completed by black, leather pants was a little distracting. Skin tight didn't touch on the extremity of the fit.

Tommy kicked the first chords off. The pub exploded in exuberant sound. The energy of the room ramped up as Tommy began to sing. James didn't know the song, but he was enjoying it.

He looked over at Corey who was grinning and clapping along to the music. James' gut clenched and his chest tightened. Corey's exuberance bordered on sublime; so much joy radiated from his face. Corey's lips sang along with the music.

James couldn't take his eyes off them.

Corey glanced over at him. His face softened and he blinked as he studied James. He looked perplexed. James turned back to watching the musician.

Their eyes had connected for far too long.

A second person wandered up to Tommy's keyboard and picked up a microphone. The performer was dressed in some kind of drag. James wasn't sure who or what he was looking at.

"Guy or girl?" he asked Corey.

"Evan Enough. Non-binary."

James exhaled. He felt like he had been dropped onto a foreign planet. But at least he knew the answer to this one.

"They-them, right?"

Corey grinned and nodded. "So, not completely sheltered."

"I try to keep up."

Evan's voice rose into the first verse while Tommy played piano. The room quietened, listening. The songs they sang, James knew. Corey was humming along, mouthing every word. James relaxed in his seat. The atmosphere in the pub felt comfortable now.

"Do you want another beer?" he asked Corey.

Corey shook his head. "No, I'm driving." He jutted his chin in the direction of the bar. "I haven't seen a server in a while. Do you want me to get you another?"

James rose to his feet. "No, I can do it. Thanks."

"Good luck."

"Ha-ha … thanks a lot."

James could feel eyes on him as he made his way over to the bar. Or, at least, he thought he could. It was unlikely anyone was looking at him. He peered over his shoulder at Corey.

Corey was tracking him. When he caught James' gaze, he smiled. A tingle ran through James' body. He exhaled to dispel it, but it was nice to know Corey was looking out for him.

He reached the bar and ordered another IPA. A few guys crowded up against him as he stood there, trying to get their orders in. One spoke to him. "You here on your own?"

James took a sip of his beer. "No, I'm here with someone."

"Lucky guy."

"Um … yeah, I guess." He could feel his cheeks redden. He cleared his throat. That shouldn't have flustered him, the guy's comment, but it did. It was a strange sensation to be hit on by a guy.

At least by someone other than Corey.

James rushed back to their table, needing to be back with Corey. His safe place for the night.

"You all right?" Corey asked.

"Yeah, sure … some guy hit on me is all."

"And you survived."

James laughed. "And I survived."

After a few more songs, Corey reached into his back pocket and withdrew his cell phone. He frowned as he looked at it. He reached across the table and tapped James' arm.

"Sorry. I have to get going. It's getting late. And this snow isn't letting up."

"Let me finish this. I'll leave with you." James tipped his glass up and drained it. It was his third beer of the evening. One in the suite. Two here. He was feeling slightly tipsy. Warm at least. He pulled on his coat and followed Corey out through the doors into the blinding snow.

"Wow …," Corey exclaimed. "It's worse than I thought out here."

James tugged his coat higher up to cover his neck and pulled up the hood. "I'll go to the parking lot with you. Help you dig out."

"You don't have to do that."

"It's the least I can do." James shoved Corey playfully. "Tonight was an eye-opener."

"In a good way?"

James sighed. "Sure, I guess so."

"Want to do it again tomorrow night? The drag show is tomorrow."

"I don't know." James tipped his head. He wanted to spend more time with Corey. "I'll make you a deal. Come snowboarding with me tomorrow and I'll join you at the pub again."

Corey grinned. "Sounds like a fantastic deal."

"I'm still not going to be your wingman."

"Agreed."

They trudged through the snow toward the *Happy Valley* parking lot. Unfortunately, the gondola was no longer running. They would have to stumble down the hill on foot. They weren't dressed for it, a trek through heavy snow. James' jeans were soaked through by the time they arrived at Corey's car— or what they could see of it. It was buried a third of the way up the doors.

"I have a brush and a shovel in the trunk," Corey said as he began brushing snow off the trunk area with his sleeve. "Might even have an extra pair of gloves."

"Appreciated." James cleared the side windows and stomped around the outline of the car. It didn't appear to be a four-wheel drive vehicle. Corey handed him a pair of gloves.

"Found some."

"Thanks." James slipped on the gloves and grabbed the brush. He started on the top of the car, clearing away the snow. Corey had a second brush and was clearing the windshield. Once they had the top of the car uncovered, they turned their attention to the wheels. Corey dug in with the shovel, trying to free up some space behind them. James concentrated on the sides of the car where they had brushed the snow onto the ground. He dropped onto his knees and shoveled the snow away from the underside with his hands. It was tough going.

After almost thirty minutes, it looked like Corey might be able to back out of his spot. James stood to one side as Corey started the vehicle, then went around to the hood, ready to push. He was shivering. His jeans were like hard sheets of ice, his thighs, and fingers numb with the cold.

A warm fire was playing on repeat in his mind.

Corey began rocking the vehicle until it gripped, but then slid back. On the next try, Corey's tires spun, spitting snow everywhere. James pushed as hard as he could, but he was running out of steam. Corey shut off the engine and pulled out his phone. James watched him through the windshield as he made call after call then appeared to give up.

James went around to the side of the vehicle as Corey hauled himself out of it.

"Guess I'm sleeping in my car." Corey held up his phone. "The mountain is booked up."

James' stomach rose in his throat, his heart hammering in his ears. The idea floating around in his head made him nervous for some reason. He pushed the feeling down.

"Don't be ridiculous. I have a comfortable sofa in my suite you can sleep on."

"Really?" Corey pulled a sports bag and his snowboarding gear out of the backseat, slammed his car door shut, and nudged James. "Thanks, buddy. I really appreciate that. I feel like an icicle. I could use a little warmth. Are you sure?"

"Positive. We'll flick the fireplace on as soon as we get back."

"Perfect."

The walk back took longer than the trip down to the parking lot. By the time they arrived at James' building, they were both shivering hard. James struggled with the lock, his hands were so numb, but they eventually managed to pile in through the door of the suite.

"Mind if I grab a hot shower?" Corey asked.

"Sure. You got clothes in that bag?"

"Yup."

"Throw your wet ones out and I'll toss them in the dryer."

"A man after my own heart."

James scowled at the floor.

"I'm joking," Corey said then closed the bathroom door behind him.

Chapter Four | Corey

The hot water felt amazing, but the fact he was naked with a simple door between him and James warmed Corey through to his core. Tossing his clothes out to James had presented him with an interesting challenge. Even though he had retained his underwear, he had opted to cover up with a towel as he opened the door a crack to pass out his wet clothes.

He concentrated on washing up. Any ideas about where the night might lead were pure delusion. He toweled off and slipped on the t-shirt and sweatpants he had thankfully left in his car last week. He ruffled up his hair, the wet curls settling on his forehead. He examined himself in the mirror. Guys found him desirable in a cheeky kind of way.

He had never had any trouble attracting attention.

Corey left the bathroom and wandered into the living room. James was hunkered down next to the roaring gas fireplace, his coat and boots discarded, still in his wet clothes.

"It's all yours ... the shower," Corey said.

"Awesome, thanks." James smiled at Corey. "Leave me any hot water?"

"Plenty." Corey caught James' arm as James walked past him. The look James gave him nearly stopped his heart. Anticipation. There was anticipation glimmering in James' eyes.

"What?" James whispered.

"Just want to know if you brought any hot chocolate. Thought I'd make us some while you're in the shower."

James visibly exhaled. "Yeah, in the grocery bag on the counter."

Corey released James' arm. "Okay. See you in a few minutes."

James gathered up his sweatshirt and sweatpants from the bedroom and disappeared into the bathroom. Corey stood near the bathroom door for a moment in case James passed out his wet clothes. He didn't. Probably afraid to open the door in any state of undress.

And whose fault was that?

Corey covered his face with his hands. He needed to pull his mind back to reality. This was going nowhere. He needed to keep reminding himself of that. That momentary glimmer in James' eyes had simply been him reacting in surprise to being grabbed.

Corey snorted out a laugh. He truly was ridiculous when it came to men. That reaffirmed, he entered the kitchen, found the hot chocolate and the kettle, and started some water boiling.

He must have been daydreaming because the kettle had clicked off and James was pushing his wet clothes into the dryer when he became aware of his surroundings again.

He removed two cups from the cupboard, dumped some hot chocolate mix into them, and added hot water. He tugged open a drawer, found a spoon, and stirred their drinks.

James leaned over the island counter and grabbed his. "Thanks for making these. The shower was great, but I feel like I'll never be warm again."

"I hear you." Corey took a seat on the sofa and closed his eyes, enjoying the heat from the fire. James plopped down beside him. Total enjoyment of the heat … and the company he was sharing it with.

"That was a good day." James took a sip of his hot chocolate. "I had some decent runs."

"You head down the bowl?"

"Twice."

Corey nodded his head. "Yeah, me too. I thought I saw you up there."

James turned in his seat. "So … you're not *out*, is that right?"

The topic change was unexpected. Corey sat up, eyeing James. It was a conversation he was willing to have. He just hadn't thought James would be interested in his story.

"Like I said, family and close friends only."

"Is that because you're embarrassed about your lifestyle?"

"Jeez, James. What kind of brainwashing has your family done on you?"

James frowned and stared down into his cup. "I'm sorry. I keep messing up." He looked at Corey. "Explain it to me … please. I want to understand."

Corey settled back in his seat, wiggling his toes in front of the flames. "First, you need to understand, I was born this way. I didn't make a choice. I didn't choose to be gay."

His gaze landed on James' expression. There was disbelief there.

"Why would I choose it?" he added. "We're persecuted, ridiculed, bullied—even killed for being queer." He warmed his hands by wrapping them around his cup.

"I was taught it was a lifestyle choice. Opting for perversion."

Corey snorted out a laugh. "What's perverted about two consenting adults finding pleasure and love with and for one another? Pretty sure your god preaches love and acceptance."

"Sometimes that gets swept under the carpet." James took

a long swallow from his cup.

"Seems to be the case."

"Are you afraid of being treated differently on the snowboarding circuit?"

Corey sighed. "I know I would be."

"Have you had many boyfriends?"

Interesting question. Changing course ever so slightly. Corey set his empty cup down on the carpet in front of the sofa. "A few. It's hard to date in the closet."

James nodded. "I've been lucky ... being that I'm straight."

"Yeah ... where is your girlfriend by the way? Is this a weekend away from her?"

James gazed into the flames. "We broke up ... she broke up with me."

"I'm sorry."

"No, it was for the best. I tried ... I tried to do everything I was supposed to."

"What do you mean?"

"We were engaged to be married."

"And that's what you were *supposed* to do?"

"According to my parents and the church."

"So, why didn't you go through with it and get married?"

James locked his attention on Corey. "It didn't feel right. Never did."

"*Right*? How do you mean by *right*?"

James shrugged. "I don't know. Ignore me." He rose to his feet. "Will this be enough for you to sleep with?" He held up an intensely furry blanket. "Or should I get you another?"

"That one will be fine. I'm going to leave the fire on."

"I'll grab you a pillow."

Corey couldn't take his eyes off James as he left the room. He could watch that man walk away a thousand times over and never grow weary of the sight. James returned with a pillow hugged against his chest, clutched tightly. He looked adorable.

"Thanks." Corey tossed the pillow onto the sofa. When he settled his face against it after they said their "Goodnights", Corey inhaled what little scent there was of James on the fabric.

He drifted off to sleep with it permeating his senses.

Chapter Five | James

Insane dreams haunted James all night long. Recounts of his day. The run with Corey—laughing, joking around—landing on him. He rubbed his eyes. His mind was playing tricks on him. They'd had a good day together. That's all it was. A little roughhousing had ensued. So what?

The few times he had climbed out of bed to get something to drink, Corey had been sound asleep on the sofa, breathing softly. During one of his trips to the kitchen, James had stood behind the sofa and watched Corey sleep. He wasn't sure what had possessed him to do so.

It was beyond creepy.

But there was something relaxing about Corey's presence.

The sleepless night wore on. While still tossing and turning, sunlight filtered into his room through the blinds. James would have hidden his face beneath his pillow and continued his attempt to sleep if the smell of coffee and bacon had not come drifting under his closed door.

He climbed out of bed, reluctantly. Four things were driving him to start his day. His need for coffee, his hunger, the call of the snow—and the thought of talking to Corey again. He pulled on some sweats, headed for the bathroom, and looked at himself in the mirror.

He looked like hell.

"Breakfast is ready," Corey called from the kitchen. He sounded chipper and well-rested. James groaned. If the guy hadn't plagued his sleep, he might've shared in Corey's morning exuberance. Typically, in his books, every day that one went snowboarding was a good day.

He wandered out of the bathroom, shielded his eyes, and peered through the living room window. Blue skies and bright sunshine. A perfect early spring day.

"Eat up so we can get out there." Corey dished up bacon, eggs, hashbrowns, and toast onto two plates. He moved aside as James pushed past him, focused on the coffee pot.

"You not sleep well?" Corey asked.

"The night was a disaster. I thought for sure I would pass out. Maybe I shouldn't have had that nap. Threw my sleep off." Lies—all of it. James sucked in a mouthful of black coffee.

"Are you going to be all right to board?" Corey asked.

James waved Corey off. "I'm fine." He lifted his plate and some utensils and headed for the table. "Thanks for making all this."

"Thanks for stocking your fridge." Corey joined him and shoveled a mouthful of egg into his mouth. He wiped the corners of his mouth with a sheet of paper towel. "I slept great."

"I might switch you for the sofa tonight."

"I'm staying another night?"

"There's no way your car is going anywhere for a while. Plus, you won't have to take off so early from watching the drag show tonight."

"I appreciate that."

"You're not working tomorrow, are you?"

Corey tipped his head and shrugged. "Nah, I took Monday off."

"Where do you work?" James lifted a piece of bacon and bit off a large chunk.

"A sporting goods store. Snowboards, skis, bicycles … you know, sports stuff. What about you?" Corey licked his fingers after sopping up some egg yolk with some toast.

"I'm a veterinary tech when I'm around. They're pretty good about giving me loads of time off when I'm competing and training. If I have a spare minute, I volunteer at an animal rescue."

Corey stopped eating; his fork poised in mid-air. "Wow. That's awesome. I love animals." He blinked at James, then went back to eating. The intensity of Corey's stare and the wonderment exuded by his eyes had James lowering his gaze and concentrating on his plate.

James ran a strip of bacon through the yellow of the egg then popped it into his mouth. Corey had done a perfect job with everything. "This is really good."

"Thanks. I like cooking."

"Yeah?" James' eyebrows rose. "Me too."

"See. A match made in heaven."

James set his fork down on his plate with a clatter. "I wish you wouldn't do that." Especially after the night he'd had with thoughts of Corey making it impossible to sleep. The teasing and innuendos were an unwelcome complication if they were going to be friends.

"I'm sorry." Corey spun his coffee cup on the table. "You're fun to tease, that's all."

"Try to keep it to yourself."

"Done."

James rose from the table and placed his dishes in the sink. The dishes from last night were on the drying rack. Corey must have washed them. He turned the hot water on. He didn't want to risk having Corey do the dishes again. Especially after he had done the cooking.

Corey stepped up beside him and slipped his plate and utensils into the sink.

"You *are* fun to tease." Corey snickered in his ear. "Your

face goes so red, and your eyes do this weird …"

James laughed and shoved Corey. "Shut it."

"Just keeping it light." Corey placed his hand at the base of James' neck and squeezed. "I don't mean anything by it." James clutched the dishcloth and pinched his eyes closed. Corey's touch sent shivers through his body. He held his breath until Corey moved away.

James closed his eyes. "I'll be done here in a second."

"I'll gear up."

"Be right behind you." James glanced over his shoulder. Corey wandered into the living room and proceeded to remove his sweatpants. He was wearing tight, thermal leggings beneath. James heaved ragged breaths in and out as he watched Corey change. He couldn't turn away.

The sunlight danced across the contours of Corey's muscular thighs.

Corey raised his head and caught James staring.

James swallowed, holding Corey's gaze, then turned back to his dishes. His mind flipped through a laundry list of reasons why Corey was fascinating him. He landed on one. He hadn't had a lot of friends growing up. His parents had preferred him to hang out with family because other people's kids were trouble. That was it. He wasn't used to being in close company with another guy his age. New territory. That's all.

He finished up the dishes and went into the bedroom to put on his snowboarding gear. He joined Corey at the front door. "Okay, let's get this snow day started."

The fresh snow was deep and glorious. The company more so. They headed straight for the bowl, wanting it to be pristine when they conquered it. Corey was of a similar mindset to him in what snowboarding meant to him. They both had a passion for it. Lived and breathed it. It was refreshing to hang out with someone that understood him.

Run after run, they kept up with each other. Their skills matched. They cascaded down a multitude of runs until they were both laughing about the fact they were overheating.

"Should we break for lunch?" Corey came to a neat stop at the bottom of the run. "My treat. It'll be my thanks for giving me a place to crash."

"I thought that's what breakfast was about."

"Hey, I didn't have to sleep in my car in wet clothes. I owe you more than breakfast."

"Just something simple. Soup and sandwich are fine."

"I know just the place."

James coasted along beside Corey, headed for the center of the village. There was a short line of people waiting on the concourse at an apparatus of some sort.

"What's that?" James pointed toward it. There were logos associated with the *Winter Pride* event covering a tall backdrop.

"Rainbow booth."

James laughed. "I'm sorry … rainbow what?"

"It's a photo booth." Corey grabbed James' sleeve and tugged him toward it. "Come on. We can have our picture taken."

James hesitated but people seemed to be having fun with it. He unfastened his board and joined Corey in the line. There was no harm in it—a picture. It wasn't until he saw people checking their phones after having their picture taken that a wave of anxiety washed over him.

These pictures went straight online.

"You all right?" Corey asked as he wrapped his arm around James' shoulders. James' initial reaction was to shrug Corey's embrace off—but he decided against it.

"I'm not sure I want to do this," he admitted.

"No one is going to see them," Corey said. "Only people that look for them on the Rainbow Booth Facebook page." He patted James' back. "If you don't want to, that's fine."

They reached the front of the line. James needed to decide. He turned to look at Corey. James sighed and chastised himself for being weak. *Damn*. The anticipation skittering across Corey's face made it impossible to refuse him. In the end, having a photo with Corey outweighed the possibility of the wrong people seeing it. He stepped in front of the camera with Corey.

After a few stupid poses, they scooted out of the way. Corey called the photos up on his phone. In two of them, Corey was staring at him, his eyelids soft, his lips slack. James' hands began to itch in his gloves as he studied them. That look ...

"Let's get out of here," he said. "Find something to eat."

After they bought sandwiches, they found a place to sit inside the lodge. They ate in silence. James chanced a few glances at Corey. It was possible Corey wanted to be more than friends. Judging by the look Corey was giving him in those photos.

James folded his cling wrap into a tidy square, his hands sweating. The realization gave James a knot in his stomach. He liked hanging out with the guy. He would hate to have to call it quits because Corey developed feelings for him.

"We still on for tonight at Pete's?" Corey asked.

"That's the plan."

"Dinner?"

"I brought stuff to make chicken curry."

Corey blinked at him. "Am I invited?"

James leveled a gaze at Corey, trying to read him. It didn't make sense to have Corey eat elsewhere. He *was* staying with him for another night. He wasn't sure why he hesitated. The thought of taking a break from Corey for dinner made him uncomfortable.

He sighed. "Only if you help me cook."

A stunning grin broke out across Corey's face. It lit up the room. James had to look away. Any longer watching Corey would have all those dreams he had been having last night resurface.

He slid off his stool. "Let's head back to the slopes."

Corey balled up his cling wrap. "Lead the way."

"Bowl again?"

"Sure … one more time."

They exited the lodge and headed for the lift. They coasted along side by side. James slid into line at the lift. "Halfpipe after that?"

"If my legs hold up."

James' mind wandered back to the morning, watching Corey change. Watching Corey's thigh muscles clench and flex as he deftly pulled on his snow pants.

His breathing quickened. A prickling heat spread over his back. Lack of sleep. Had to be. After a good night's sleep, his thoughts would return to normal.

He piled into a lift chair with Corey.

Corey breathed in a deep breath beside him. "Do you want kids?"

James blinked. Out of left field, or what? He turned in his seat to face Corey. "Someday." He unzipped his coat. The sun was heating things up. "With the right person."

"Yeah." Corey nodded. "Me too."

James screwed up his face. "But … "

"What?" Corey crossed his arms. "You think because I'm

gay, I can't have kids?"

"No, I'm sure there are ways to do that. I just didn't think you would want any."

"Why?"

"For reasons I am going to keep my mouth shut about." James shoved Corey's shoulder gently. "It would get me in trouble. And I'm positive I'm totally wrong about it."

"You're learning."

James settled back in his seat. "I think you would make a great dad."

Corey patted James' thigh. "Thanks. You too."

James grunted and prepared to dismount the lift. Kids. When he got home, his mom would likely set him up with another *nice girl* from church. Regardless of the rumors, he would make another attempt at it. Maybe before the year was out, he would be engaged again. Then married. Then there would be children. And life would become normal. Plodding along … normal.

Corey whooped as he dismounted and slid down the ramp. James chased after him. He pounded Corey on the back when he caught up. Any weirdness between them earlier was forgotten. Their love of their sport overshadowed everything. The brilliant expanse of snow beckoned to them. They caught each other's eye, grinning, and took off down the slope.

Chapter Six | Corey

Corey hadn't been able to stop himself, staring at James as they had their pictures taken. James' smile was heart-wrenching. The discomfort James displayed when they looked at the pictures spoke volumes. James wasn't interested. He needed to cut it out, falling over himself to attract James' interest. Feeding off every bit of attention James gave him.

A romance wasn't happening.

Corey adjusted his board; prepared to make another run at one of the jumps. James was waiting for him at the bottom. This was their last run. The air he caught was epic. His form was perfect as he completed a backflip and landed it with precision.

James was laughing and clapping as Corey sped toward the fence.

"Nice air." James pounded him on the back and hauled Corey into an embrace; one arm around Corey's shoulders. It was almost too much to bear. The contact. What he would give to have James' arms wrapped around his body, protecting him from the world.

Their time together, talking and snowboarding had solidified things for him. He was crushing hard on James. And there were hints of other emotions bubbling beneath the surface.

Corey's eyes nearly teared up. He was setting himself up for some serious heartache.

"Curry," James said.

Corey managed a smile. "Let's do it."

The trip back to the condo was slower than Corey would

have liked. He wanted to be back there, just the two of them. Cooking and talking—laughing together. The sun was hanging low in the sky when they finally made their way to the condos.

After changing into their sweats, James lifted some chicken out of the fridge. They worked easily together. Each took on a task without much communication other than the easy flow of conversation and ridiculous banter filling every corner of the kitchen.

They tucked up on the sofa and dug into the curry they had made.

"We could have made it hotter," Corey said.

"Next time."

Corey tipped his head to one side. *Next time?* Was this going to turn into a regular thing? Going away on snowboarding weekends together? He stopped eating. His heart was pounding in his chest. He couldn't do that. He wouldn't continue to torture himself like that.

He remained silent.

James looked at him. "I didn't mean to assume anything. I just thought we could do this again sometime."

"No … yeah. Sure."

James frowned. "You don't want to."

"I never said that."

James set his plate on the floor. "I thought we were having fun."

"It's more complicated than that." Corey scrapped his fork back and forth through the curry left on his plate. He looked up and met James' gaze. "I've been enjoying this *too* much."

A rush of crimson rose in James' cheeks. "You like me."

Corey abandoned his plate on the floor. "Can I be honest with you?"

"I'm not sure." James pulled the throw blanket into his lap.

"But go ahead."

Corey exhaled. "I've had a crush on you for years. I plowed into you deliberately in the lift line. I had this crazy idea that hanging out with you … that it might go somewhere."

"I'm not gay, Corey."

"I know. I know." Corey smiled. "A boy can dream, though, right?"

"I don't know what to say."

"Say you still want to be friends. That we have that at least." If James ditched him now, he might never recover. It would be easier on his heart if James did slough him off, but deep down, Corey couldn't bear the thought of never hanging out with him again like this. But weekends away together. Those were out of the question.

James furrowed his brow. "I need to lie down before we get ready to go to Pete's" He rose to his feet. "Alone. We'll leave it at that. I don't want to discuss this anymore."

Chapter Seven | James

He might not want to discuss it with Corey, but his mind certainly wanted to plague him with the implications of what Corey had said. And what might have been said if he had stuck around to hear more. Sleep did not come to him at all. Corey's admission of attraction to him; a crush. That Corey had been crushing on him for years. The very idea floored him.

He rolled over, clutched his spare pillow to his chest, and exhaled the breath he had been holding. Where did they go from here? Surely, this would make things awkward between them.

James opened his eyes and looked at the wall. The thought of ditching Corey caused him an unfathomable amount of distress. He hadn't had this much fun with anyone in a long time. His mind rolled through images of how their friendship might endure.

He flipped onto his back and covered his face with both hands. He rubbed his eyes. He wanted this. He wanted to continue his friendship with Corey. Corey's attraction to him would have to be buried. Over time, Corey would forget about his feelings. Right?

He righted himself, planted his feet on the floor, and roughed up his hair. Maybe they could go early to Pete's. Start the night off with a few drinks before the drag queens took the stage. Having a warm buzz on sounded like the answer to his discomfort.

Corey was asleep on the sofa when he entered the living

room. He hated to disturb him. His steady reassuring breaths filled the space. His cheeks were rosy from the cold.

James sighed as he leaned over the back of the sofa.

Damn. The temptation to brush his knuckles across that crimson skin was strong.

He shut the image out of his mind. The urge to start a night of drinking diverted the direction of his thoughts. He reached down and touched Corey's shoulder. When Corey didn't rouse, he gave his shoulder a slight shake. Corey's eyes fluttered open, and he smiled up at James. His features were soft and sleepy. The word *angelic* popped into James' mind.

James grunted, wiping yet another random train of thought clean out of his head. "Do you mind if we head out early? I need a proper drink. I only have beer here."

Corey clutched the back of the sofa and sat up. "Fine by me." He leaned over his duffel bag. "Hey, could I borrow a sweater from you? I've kinda run out of clothes."

"Sure, yeah." James went into his bedroom and lifted the cream cable-knit sweater he'd been wearing the night before off his bed. It would look good on Corey.

Corey's eyes lit up when he saw it. "Nice. Thanks."

After changing into their outerwear, they walked silently across the square to Pete's. The wind had returned but not the snow. It was a beautiful clear night. James took a moment to look up into the sky at the stars before stepping through the door into a new experience.

Corey led the way into the pub, headed straight for an empty table near the stage area. This put them in the direct line of fire if Trixie Lamour took the stage again.

James slung his coat over the back of the chair, resigned. Corey was visibly excited to have found a table so close to the action.

"What's your poison tonight," Corey asked, rubbing his hands together.

"What are you having?"

"Gin and tonic." Corey winked at him. "Gotta watch my figure."

A rush of warmth rippled from James' abs into his chest. It nearly choked off his breath. It seemed the teasing was going to continue. He emitted a strangled, "I'll have the same."

"I'll grab the first round."

"Right ... sure."

This time James couldn't take his eyes off Corey as he strolled to the bar. James' chest heaved; ragged breaths dragged back and forth across his parted lips. He was warm all over.

He licked his lips.

Corey looked back at him from the bar. The look of longing on Corey's face persisted until the bartender caught Corey's attention. James looked down at the tabletop. Any thoughts of Corey burying his feelings for him seemed ludicrous. There was no way he was going to cut Corey loose, though. Every moment he spent in Corey's company was amazing. He was at peace. He was exhilarated. His world made sense. This was a friendship he wanted to keep.

"Here you go." Corey set the gin and tonic in front of him. "I made the executive decision to start the night off with doubles." A smirk of anticipation joined by a wink followed.

James nodded. "I'm in full agreement." He lifted his glass. "To my first drag show."

Corey laughed as he brought his glass to touch James'. "To many firsts."

James snorted out a laugh. "Don't get any crazy ideas." He kept his attention on Corey as he took a sip of his drink. It was cool against his lips. Corey didn't look away.

Corey broke eye contact with him and took a gulp of his drink, then drained it. The ice rattled inside his glass as he set it on the table. "Another?"

James chuckled. "So that's how it's going to be. I'm in." He finished the earthy taste of the gin and gathered up Corey's glass. "My round."

Standing at the bar, James was much more comfortable than he had been the night before. The place wasn't crowded yet and no one came on to him. He ordered a couple more doubles and headed back to the table. Corey was chatting with someone. The guy was muscular, dark-haired, and classically handsome. He had his hand on Corey's shoulder and was caressing it.

A knot settled in James' stomach.

James squeezed past the guy, set the drink in front of Corey, and took his seat. Without thinking, he raised his eyebrows at the guy. Kind of a "What the hell do you think you're doing?" expression. He was here with Corey tonight. His friend could pick up guys some other time.

The guy took the message, said, "Nice meeting you," to Corey, and wandered off.

"Nice cock block," Corey said, barely containing a smile.

"You promised me I wouldn't be your wingman. I take that role seriously."

"Didn't know that meant you'd be my protector."

James shrugged. "That's what friends do. Look out for each other."

"Yeah, I guess." Corey scowled at the tabletop and took a swig of his drink. He set his glass down and released a heavy sigh. He looked up at James. "How does the next year look for you?"

A welcome shift of gears. Away from the personal stuff.

James twirled his glass on the table. "I figure I only have a couple of years left in me. Gonna push hard preparing for next season."

Corey nodded. "Same." He lifted his glass and held it to his lips until there was only ice left. There was every chance Corey was going to drink him under the table tonight.

By the time the drag show started, they were five doubles in each. Corey decided it was time to switch to shots. James didn't argue. The drinks, the exuberance of the crowd, and being in Corey's company spread warmth through him.

Corey was ecstatic each time a new performer took the stage. The joy on Corey's face was captivating. And Corey's clapping, whistling, and cheering put a vice grip on James' chest.

Trixie Lamour made the rounds during his performance, giving men lap dances and standing behind others, running his fingers through their hair.

"He's good," James yelled at Corey, attempting to be heard above the loud music.

Corey leaned toward him and touched James' hand. "She."

"What?"

"You call a drag queen *she*."

"Oh, sure … okay."

Corey withdrew his hand and went back to cheering on Trixie's performance. James drew his hand into a fist. For a moment, the heat of Corey's hand had been on his. Now, the ghost of the sensation lingered. And he craved it. Craved more of it.

He headed to the bar for more shots.

Chapter Eight | Corey

The night was confusing him. James was confusing him. James was adamant he was straight, but he had caught James staring at him a few times. At the condo … at the bar. And not just staring. James was staring with a level of hunger. Hunger and anticipation.

Of course, he might have been imagining things.

Corey threw back the shot James brought to the table. A Jägerbomb. The combination of Jägermeister and Red Bull made his head swim and his imagination surge. He moved his chair to be closer to James'. James didn't appear to mind. He just peered over at him and went back to watching the show. Corey held his breath and knocked his knee up against James' under the table.

This was insanity. His mind knew it. His heart knew it. His drunken ass didn't.

The firm press of James' knee back against Corey's nearly knocked the breath out of him. Maybe it was involuntary. Maybe James didn't know he was doing it.

God … so many maybes.

James shifted in his seat, increasing the pressure against Corey's knee. There was no mistaking the intention behind that move. Corey pretended to be interested in the latest drag queen's performance. But his exuberance for the art had been overshadowed.

The moment was broken when Ieata Cox set her sights on James. She spun his chair to face her and straddled his lap. She danced and ground on him, then abandoned him, headed for her next victim. James, red-faced, shuffled his chair back to face the table.

"You all right?" Corey could barely contain the giggle threatening to erupt from his throat at James' expense. He reached down and put his hand on James' thigh.

James flinched.

Too much.

James leaped up from his seat. "One more?" He pointed at the empty shot glasses.

"Sure." After James left the table and headed for the bar, Corey lowered his head onto his crossed arms on the table. Shit—shit—shit. He'd pushed James too hard.

"Fuck," he whispered against his arms. What the hell was he playing at? James was straight. Straight and drunk. He knew better than to toy with that potential firestorm.

"Here." James nudged his shoulder and placed the shot in front of him. Corey peered up from his arms at it. This would the last one. He was tired, horny, and wasted. Best to call it a night and head for bed—alone. There would be plenty of time to beat himself up for accosting James in the morning during what would likely be an epic hangover.

"Throw it back and we'll go," James echoed.

The shot barely made it past his lips. He was finished. His legs would likely deceive him when he tried to stand. He clutched the edge of the table and attempted the maneuver.

All good. His legs held.

Corey slipped on his coat and followed James out through the door. It was probably cold outside, but he could barely feel it. He stumbled along behind James across the square. He wondered if their friendship was going to survive the foolish assumption he had made.

He had wanted it so bad ... but he had misread the signals.

The suite was dark as they trudged through the door. Corey found the wall, leaning against it to remove his boots. He could sense James was close. He didn't dare touch him again. Corey made sure to give James plenty of room as he made his way around him into the living room.

He flicked on the fireplace.

The warm firelight filled the room. He slid onto the floor, resting his back against the front of the sofa. He just needed a few minutes for his head to stop spinning, then he'd lie down.

He was startled when James sunk onto the floor beside him.

"Drank too much," James said.

"Understatement."

"Sorry I scared that guy off."

"What guy?"

"The guy that was hitting on you."

"Oh, him. Yeah ... not really my type."

"You got something against tall, dark, and handsome?" A soft snort accompanied the question, joined by James leaning his shoulder against Corey's.

"I prefer blonds," Corey whispered. And this particular blond, James, would never be his. He tipped his head until it was touching James'. It felt nice.

"Right," James replied.

Corey could see James' chest rise and fall dramatically next to him.

"I prefer brown and curly," James whispered ever so softly.

Corey's pulse thundered through his body. That was a signal. A definite signal. He hadn't been mistaken. James *was* interested. He reached for James' thigh, chancing a second rejection. This time, James' warm hand covered his, and James' fingers slipped through the spaces of Corey's, joining their hands in an embrace of sorts.

"James," Corey whispered.

"Yes … yes, I do." James turned his face. His breath fluttered past Corey's ear. The fingers of James' free hand brushed across Corey's exposed cheek. So incredibly gentle and tentative.

Corey just about wept.

Chapter Nine | James

The sight of Corey sitting on the floor, the firelight dancing on his hair—it had obliterated his resolve to stay angry at him. James slumped down onto the carpet beside Corey. He leaned against him. There it was. Physical connection with Corey felt intense; unprecedented.

He wasn't surprised to hear Corey hadn't been interested in the guy hitting on him. His body language had been off; his intense light had been dimmed. So unlike when Corey was with him.

"I prefer blonds," Corey whispered.

James knew those words were meant for him. Hearing them—a fierce battle erupted within him. There was a longing for Corey. He could feel it. He wanted to deny it, but it pulled at him.

Just say it.

His heart thundered in his chest.

"I prefer brown and curly."

Speaking those words terrified him. He hadn't recognized his admiration was attraction until Corey had touched his hand in the pub. He'd been snowblind to the possibility. He had confirmed his suspicion by pressing his knee against Corey's under the table.

It had flooded his system with desire.

Corey's hand came to rest on his thigh. So gentle. James needed reassurance from his friend. That what came next was going to be all right. That he was safe and protected. He entwined his fingers with Corey's and clung to them. It brought him the calm he sought.

"James."

"Yes … yes, I do."

Yes, I do … I really like you and desperately want to kiss you.

James turned and nuzzled Corey's ear with his nose. The scent of Corey's hair tickled James' senses, warm and earthy. He wanted to inhale every bit of him. Body and soul. He reached for Corey's face and angled it toward him. The dusting of bristles on Corey's jaw thrilled him.

James freed his face from Corey's hair.

His lips—he needed Corey's lips.

A shudder ran through him as their lips met. So soft and warm. Tender, gentle kisses. Each one increased in intensity. An ebb and flow as their mouths explored one another. The exchange of warm breath—the sighing—the hunger. Every kiss so incredibly bound by desire.

James shifted his body, wrapped his hand around the back of Corey's neck, and tugged him closer. He needed Corey firmly against him. Needed to envelop him—possess him. Corey rose on his knees and lowered James onto the carpet on his back. For the second time in two days, they found their bodies pressed together. This time, James had no intention of struggling away.

One hand on the back of Corey's head, the other on his broad shoulders, James deepened the kiss. He released Corey's mouth, moaning, as Corey ground against him with his hips. Corey's cock was thick and firm, prodding and teasing. James undulated up to meet him, rock hard.

Corey gasped in James' mouth.

James grabbed Corey's ass, tugging him tight against his

body.

"Wait," Corey whispered and pulled away. "James, wait …" He pressed a hand to James' chest. "We shouldn't be doing this. We're drunk."

"So."

James tried to sneak another kiss, but Corey kept out of his reach. The distance was maddening. He wanted the closeness back again. The kissing and grinding—and more.

He wanted so much more. He never could have imagined he'd ever have such a gut-twisting ache for a guy. That he would want to feel his skin. Stroke it—caress it—taste it.

"You might regret this in the morning, James."

"Nah … I'm good."

James wrinkled his brow. It was possible Corey was right. He had never *been* with anyone before. The church did not allow sex before marriage. He had stuck to that diligently his entire adult life. He certainly knew what they would have to say about same-sex … sex.

But surely it would be different with Corey. It would be pure and good. He could feel it. How could anyone object to that?

Corey chuckled. "You're *good* all right." He reached back for the blanket on the sofa and shuffled down until he was resting his head on James' chest then covered them both.

"Hold me," Corey hummed against James' chest.

James wrapped his arms around Corey's body and hugged him. Corey snuggled in against James' shoulder and closed his eyes.

The peace was sublime. James released a relaxed breath. This would have to do. And that was fine by him. He had Corey in his arms.

James opened his eyes far too early in his estimation. His head was spinning, and he had a vicious headache. The chance of throwing up was not out of the question. Corey murmured something in his sleep beside him. He was tucked against James' chest, still laying on his arm.

James adjusted the blanket to ensure Corey was covered then tipped his chin and kissed Corey on the head. The scent of him filled James' psyche. He stared up at the ceiling.

Tears. His eyes were tearing up.

The contentment he felt was startling.

Corey had been right to stop them last night. James wasn't ready. He had only just realized his fascination with Corey was attraction. He needed to reconcile that with his faith before they had any chance of creating something special. The spark was there. A spark that could lead to something wonderful. He could feel it in his heart.

"James." Corey snuggled deeper into James' embrace. "I don't feel so good. Can I just lie here forever? We could have food brought to us." Corey groaned. "Ugh … food. That's the last thing I need. Aspirin would be an awesome choice, though."

"I might have some in my bag."

"That means you'd have to move." Corey placed his arm across James' chest. "I'll suffer."

"Corey." James touched Corey's face and brushed some hair off his forehead. "When do you think we'll see each other again?"

Corey peered up at him. "Next week at the winter games?"

"I hadn't planned on going but I *am* registered."

"So, it's a date."

James shook his head. "My parents are planning to come with me if I go."

"We could find some time to spend together. They don't follow you around, do they?"

James snorted. "A little bit, yeah."

"Then I'll have to kidnap you." Corey smiled up at James, then kissed his chest.

James rolled Corey onto his back and hovered over him. He settled a soft kiss on Corey's lips, pulled away, and stared into Corey's eyes. "I'd like that."

Corey ran his hand into the thick hair at the back of James' head and clung to him.

"Please do that again," he whispered.

James pressed his lips to Corey's, tasting—teasing. He hummed against them, caught up in the precious intimacy between them. It was going to be agony to be away from Corey for a whole week. He wanted to snowboard, laugh, and cook together again. Their time at the Winter Games would be fleeting at best. But they'd have to make the most of it. He might even chance his parents' disappointment and disappear overnight. He was a grown man after all.

It wouldn't be enough. He wanted more.

"I want to plan a weekend away with you," James said. "Could you get the time off?"

Corey brushed his thumb across James' bottom lip. "For you … anything."

Chapter Ten | Corey

Waking up in James' arms was everything Corey had dreamed it would be. Strong and solid—warm. Encasing him like he was the most precious thing in the world. Corey sighed. The gentle kiss James had placed on his head while James thought he was asleep was beyond his imagination.

He stroked his fingers up and down James' sweater, wishing they'd had some skin contact last night. Laying on James' bare chest would have been heart-stopping. He shifted and kissed James' neck. James hummed in response. This was glorious, lying here.

James grunted and covered his face with his hand. "I have to pee."

Well, that's the end of that.

"Yeah, me too." Corey pushed himself up on one arm. He clutched James' bicep when the room did a series of loop-dee-loops. "Whoa. Not good. Note to self … shots—bad."

"Agreed."

James sat up, rolled to his knees, and clambered to his feet. He reached out to help Corey. Once on his feet, James pulled Corey into his arms. It felt incredible, to hold each other. Their bodies molded together. Their hearts beat strong; their rhythms distinct but unified.

"God … this feels good," Corey whispered in James' ear.

"That's what he said." James' chest rumbled as he laughed. Corey pulled away, enjoying the ease between them. This morning could have been awkward. Or heartbreaking. James might have woken up and regretted everything and bolted. Instead, James was staying right here with him.

"Now, you're learning." Corey touched James' cheek. "You are so beautiful."

James smirked. "No one has ever called me that before."

"You are … inside and out. I can tell."

"Well, this beautiful guy is going to pee himself in a second."

Corey laughed and stepped out of the way so James could make his way to the bathroom. In the interest of his throbbing head, he went in search of water. Thankfully, the cold water tap supplied him with a large glass of ice-cold relief. He pressed the glass against his head between gulps. As soon as James exited the bathroom, he bolted past him to take his turn.

After washing his hands, he opened the cabinet over the sink. Aspirin.

Oh, thank God.

He popped the bottle open, dumped two out into his hand, and swallowed them with a bit of water from the tap. He guessed James would want some too, so he took the bottle into the kitchen with him. James was leaning over the kitchen sink, using his cupped hand to drink water.

"You all right?" Corey placed his hand on James' back and rubbed the firm expanse between James' shoulder blades. He rattled the aspirin bottle. "These might help."

"That and sleep." James grabbed the bottle and took two tablets.

"Should I go?" Corey hoped not, but if James wanted to be alone and sleep this hangover off, he could attempt to drive himself home. After sleeping on the floor last night, lying in a proper bed felt like what his body needed right now.

James looked at him with a hint of desperation in his eyes.

"Do you have to go?" he asked.

"Do you want me to stay?"

James reached for Corey's face and cupped his cheek. "You have no idea how much."

Climbing into bed with James sounded glorious. Maybe stripping down to their underwear. Maybe more. Could he trust himself to lie beside James and not make a move on him? He sensed James needed more time before they moved this connection between them into something sexual.

It was better if he left.

"My dog sitter is expecting me back this morning."

"You have a dog?" The disappointment in James' eyes was accompanied by light.

"Two. Golden Retrievers. They keep me sane."

"How do you find time to be their human?"

"It's hard. I'm away so much, but my sitter is great."

James licked his lips and stepped closer. He used the hand cupping Corey's cheek to draw him near. "You're the beautiful one." Then James kissed him—hard and deep.

Corey felt it in his toes.

It was a man demanding more from him.

His resolve crumbled. Corey clutched the back of James' head to increase the pressure on his lips. James' tongue slid into his mouth, a man possessed, and nearly undid him. He met him there, spearing his tongue between James' lips. His taste was heady—intoxicating.

When James pulled at Corey's clothes, shuffling Corey across the room toward the bedroom, he didn't have a single objection left in him. It seemed James didn't need extra time to do any soul-searching after all. Without losing connection with his lips, James had him in the bedroom, his hands searching for a way into Corey's clothes.

Corey pushed away and peeled his shirt off over his head. James did the same. James' sweater landed on the floor. They stood for a brief moment—eyes perusing. Chests heaving. Then collided—lips seeking—hands grabbling with belts and buckles.

Corey's dreams had never achieved this level of passion. The most he had wished for was having James take a risk and kiss him. Maybe hold him.

James stripped the belt from Corey's pants.

They were really doing this.

Corey turned James and pushed him down onto the unmade bed: looking up at Corey, his feet still on the floor. Corey dropped to his knees and wrestled with James' belt and fly. Successful, he yanked James' pants off his hips, underwear, and all. He was met with a fierce, hard cock.

It was in his mouth before he had a chance to think about it.

The groan James emitted was like music. Every nerve in his body responded to it. Ecstasy. James raked his fingers into Corey's hair, clutching—grasping. Corey used one hand to steady James' cock, and the other to grip his thigh. Every pass along James' shaft with his mouth sent a stream of rumbling groans through James' lips.

James' hand soon clawed at his head.

"Fuck, Corey ... I'm ..."

Corey reached for James' hand and held it. The grip returned came in pulses, bursts of strength. Until James' body stilled. Corey released James' cock and licked his lips.

He'd be riding on the high of that experience all the way home.

As Corey rose to his feet, James kicked his pants off and onto the ground. He shuffled up the bed until he was fully on it, his bare skin cradled by the pure white sheets.

All Corey could do was stand and stare.

Gorgeous.

Chapter Eleven | James

James had to smile. Corey was just standing there at the side of the bed, staring with his mouth open. It gave him a boost in confidence. James tucked himself under the duvet and flipped open one side. His breath caught and he gripped his pillow as Corey stripped off his jeans and underwear. Now it was his turn to stare. Corey's muscles were like sculpted marble. Smooth and hard. And his cock—he'd only ever seen other men naked in changing rooms. Not aroused.

Corey was stunning.

His heart thudded in his chest. He needed to touch him.

He reached for Corey's hand, motioning for him to join him. Corey took his hand, his tight grip a plea for reassurance. He climbed into the bed and covered them both with the duvet. They lay face to face on one pillow, sharing their warm breath.

Corey brushed his hand down James' cheek and kissed him. Each kiss was gentle and filled with a mix of desperation and affection. The man before him knew he needed a moment.

James broke contact. "What do I do?" He touched Corey's chin. "I don't know what to do." Any kind of sex was unknown territory for him, but this … this was absolutely foreign. He wanted to bring Corey as much pleasure as Corey had done for him.

"Here." Corey took James' hand and guided it down his body, deep beneath the covers. Down past his chest and his abs. James exhaled and bit his bottom lip. Corey's cock was warm and hard—and velvety soft—so incredibly soft. James wrapped his hand around it.

"Just do what feels good to you," Corey said.

James pulled gently, keeping his grip firm. Corey closed his eyes, his lips slack. Again—and again, he guided Corey's cock through his hand.

"James …" Corey kissed him. "That's it …" He gasped—licked his lips, his hips pumping forward into James' hand. Every sound Corey made was pure and heavenly. James wanted to capture that sound to keep with him forever. It was a sound that needed to be kept near his heart.

Corey's body rocked back and forth. James held steady, watching Corey—his eyes, fluttering—his mouth; tongue licking lips. James couldn't take his eyes off him.

"James … James …"

Pulse—release. Thrusting and retreating. Time and again. Corey's body shuddered through each surge until he melted against James, panting. It was the most intimate experience James had ever had with anyone. It couldn't have been with anyone else. It felt so right with Corey.

James smiled against Corey's lips as Corey kissed him. He was where he was supposed to be. There was no denying it.

"What are you smiling about?" Corey pulled away and smiled back at him.

"I'm happy."

"So am I" Corey brushed his fingers across James' lips. "You surprised me last night. Initiating that kiss. I thought my heart was going to beat out of my chest."

"I'm surprised I didn't have a heart attack."

Corey kissed James' nose. "I'm glad you didn't."

James sat up, reached toward the end of the bed, and grabbed a used towel. He cleaned his hand off and handed the towel to Corey. Once Corey was finished with it, he tossed it onto the floor, cuddled back under the covers, and rolled over to place his back against James' chest.

"I need sleep," Corey said.

"Agreed." James threw his arm over Corey's body and tugged him close. He nestled his face at the back of Corey's head, letting the scent of the man he'd come to trust more than any other lull him off to sleep. The world would still be there in a few hours.

James chuckled to himself. He'd awoken to Corey grinding his ass back against his hard post-nap wood. He moved his hand down onto Corey's abs, then onto his pubes, his knuckles brushing beneath Corey's rock-hard cock. He rubbed his thumb back and forth on Corey's skin.

"Oh, good … you're awake," Corey said.

"Was that your plan?"

Corey laughed. "Maybe."

James gripped Corey's cock. It was firm and tight. He pumped it a few times then rolled his thumb over the tip. It was slick. So incredibly slick. He just about came. To have this effect on a guy—a guy he cared for; was beyond comprehension. It gave him shivers.

He thrust his cock along the base of Corey's spine, then shuffled closer. It took a great deal of concentration to continue thrusting while stroking Corey's cock with any kind of rhythm.

"Taking everything into your own hands this afternoon." Corey reached back and placed his hand on James' hip to encourage him. They undulated in unison—moaning and sighing.

James needed to taste him.

He sucked and tongued Corey's shoulder and teased the skin with his teeth.

Corey groaned and tipped his head back.

"God … James."

James closed in on Corey's neck. His neck, his shoulder—behind his ear. Nibbling his ear lobe. "I want you to cum for me." Okay, he'd watched a few porn videos. He knew some lingo.

Corey laughed. "So demanding."

The sheets were damp and warm as the intensity increased. Rocking perfectly together as if joined. Corey was the first to release the tension. James soon after.

They dissolved into a mound of sweaty bodies. After a moment of acrobatics, Corey managed to retrieve the dirty towel from the floor. He handed it to James and settled back at James' side. James carefully wiped the evidence of their passion from Corey's skin.

"I love waking up like that," Corey said.

"First time for me … but I loved it."

"Wait … what?" Corey rolled over to face James.

"You've never had sex after a nap before?"

James scrubbed a hand across his face. "No." He set his hand on Corey's shoulder. "Can I be honest with you?"

"Always."

"I've never had sex before."

"Wait." Corey rose on one elbow. "Like never … never."

"Never."

"I'm your first?" Corey's eyebrows rose. "You're a virgin?"

"Is that a problem?"

Corey leaned forward and kissed him. "Not at all. I just wish you had told me."

"It's embarrassing."

"Is that a church thing again?"

"Yeah, no sex before marriage."

"Well, you just blew that one of the water. Twice."

James grinned. "And I don't even feel guilty about it."

"I should hope not." Corey looked into James' eyes and smiled. "Are you sure you're all right? You just burned some serious bridges there."

"I'm more than all right. You're special. I've never felt like this about anyone. I'm so comfortable with you. We have so much in common. We just clicked."

"We did, didn't we." Corey tapped James' chin. "I have a lot of respect for you. You're an awesome competitor. An incredible guy. My crush on you was justified. I want you to know that."

"Noted." James kissed Corey. "I need a shower."

"Yeah, me too. Mind if I join you?"

Mind?

After what they'd already shared, James was ready for anything and everything new. He threw the duvet off, climbed out of bed, and reached for Corey's hand.

Corey stepped into the shower first after the temperature was agreed upon. James liked his shower on the hot side—Corey on the cool. They compromised. James wandered in behind Corey and wrapped his arms around Corey's body and kissed the back of his neck. The water made Corey's skin slick and smooth beneath his lips.

He could have held that pose forever.

James turned Corey to face him and kissed him gently. Warm water flowed over their joined lips. Corey moved his hands over James' hips and onto his ass. James released Corey's mouth to let them both catch a breath. He enveloped Corey in his arms and held him, enjoying the feel of Corey's hands caressing his ass. His grip was strong—demanding.

James slid his hands down Corey's back, over his ass, and

onto his thighs. An urge pulled at him—daring him—demanding to be sated. Obedient, he sunk onto his knees.

"James, you don't have to …"

James kissed Corey's hip bone. "I want to."

He lifted Corey's soft cock with one thumb and dragged his tongue across Corey's balls. They were delicate and furry. He tipped his chin and sucked one into his mouth. He moaned as it settled on his tongue, warm and wet. He circled the tip of his tongue around the sac, then sucked, tugged, and released it. He grinned and gave the other equal treatment.

He couldn't imagine doing this with anyone else.

"Jeez, James." Corey touched James' head.

James looked up. Corey's wet lashes gave them a sexy, inky quality around pools of blue. Tendrils of curly, dark hair framed his face. Rivulets of water ran down his cheeks.

Corey was gorgeous.

"Come back to my mouth," Corey whispered. James rose to his feet and dove into the increasingly familiar ecstasy of Corey's lips. He pressed Corey against the wall of the shower stall. Their abs and chests heaved—no space between them. Breathing as one.

Corey broke free from James' mouth and laughed. He entwined his fingers with James' and spun him to change places. "Okay, tiger, I really do have to get going."

James pouted dramatically. "Yeah, check-out was like hours ago."

"Soap and shampoo each other?"

"Yum … yes, please."

"You're incorrigible."

"I like what I like."

"And you *like* me."

"You haven't figured that out yet?"

Corey grinned. "Just checking."

James' admiration had turned into so much more. An intense connection. Corey had to know how much he liked him. After years in the church, it felt like life was finally opening up for him.

Chapter Twelve | Corey

Corey was glad James had agreed to let him drop him off at the airport. It had given them more time to spend together. More time to talk. More time to share about their lives. And now that they had taken a really important step for James, it was nice to be able to discuss the sexual stuff. What it meant to James. What it meant to him. How it had all happened so quickly.

He felt secure in the way they had left things. James had given him a quick kiss in the car before dashing for the departure doors. They had almost been late for James' flight. The soap and shampoo had led to other things. They both had voracious sexual appetites.

Corey smirked, laughing, then sighed, deflated.

James had made him promise one thing. That he wouldn't tell anyone about them. If Corey mentioned a new guy he was seeing, James' name was never to come up. It was the same arrangement Corey had demanded of other men he'd been dating in the past.

Now he knew what it felt like to have your existence denied.

He wanted to shout from the rooftops that he was seeing James Cartwright. That the man of his dreams wanted to be with him and ravish him every chance he got.

Corey gripped his steering wheel. The entire weekend had been like a dream. The snowboarding, the cooking, the hanging out at Pete's, listening to music—watching drag.

That first kiss.

Corey rolled his eyes. Damn, that had been good. James' hesitation as he worked up the nerve to take his mouth had been tantalizing. It made his stomach flutter thinking of it. He would've taken bets on James changing his mind; too scared to take what he so obviously wanted.

It had taken a lot of courage on James' part. Especially with his background. What was a good church boy doing kissing a boy anyway?

Corey grinned. *Making some serious moves on me, that's what.*

He pulled into the driveway of the house where he rented a basement apartment. He hefted his duffel bag and snowboard to the door and knocked. He didn't want to bother struggling to retrieve his keys. Kala would still be there. He'd given her a recap of his weekend by text. She wanted to know the details. All of them. Little sisters—some things never changed.

"Hey, big bro!" Kala pulled the snowboard out of his hand. With her free hand, she grabbed his arm and hauled him into the living room. "Come on … tell all."

Corey tossed his bag onto the sofa. "Give me a sec." He dropped onto one knee as two boisterous golden retrievers bounded out of his bedroom. "Gotta say hello to my boys."

"Syd and Gus were dears. The whole weekend."

"Did those drops work for Syd's ears?" Corey bent back the ear of one dog and looked inside. He'd had a lot of gunk building up in them.

"They're looking better, don't you think?" Kala ruffled the fur on Syd's head.

"A lot cleaner." He looked up at his sister. "Thanks, Kala … again."

"All worth it if my brother spills." She plopped down on

the sofa. "Sit. Tell all."

"Fine." Corey sat beside her. "I met a guy."

"Yes, I know that part. What happened?"

"We snowboarded a lot. He loves it as much as I do. Maybe even more."

"And …"

"We cooked curry together. He loves cooking too."

"And …"

"We went to Winter Pride. Watched a musician. Saw a drag show."

"And …"

"And then he kissed me in front of the fireplace back at his suite."

Kala shoved Corey's shoulder. "Was it good?"

Corey grinned. "So good." He ducked his gaze and stared at his hands.

"There's more." Kala gripped his arm and shook it. "Tell me."

"We may have ended up in bed together. Twice. And again, in the shower."

Kala pounded Corey's thigh. "You really like him, don't you?"

"Yeah. A lot." Corey sighed. "More than I should."

"What do you mean?"

"I've been crushing on the guy for a while. Never thought we'd end up together."

"Wait … it's not …" Kala smacked Corey's arm. "Not James."

The look gave it away. He couldn't contain the level of glee he was feeling. He was giddy. Truly. It wasn't a secret from his sister that he'd had a crush on James. Kala had bugged him endlessly about it over the years. His sister would have to keep it to herself, though.

Corey nodded. "But you can't tell anyone. He doesn't want anyone to know."

"Who would I tell?" She looked like the Cheshire Cat, grinning.

"I'm serious, Kala. I promised him I wouldn't tell anyone. His family is super Christian. Plus, neither one of us wants to have our personal lives *out* there on the circuit."

"I get it. I've never slipped with any of your other relationships. You know you can trust me."

Corey patted her leg. "Thanks, Kala." He dug into his pocket. His phone had buzzed. He tapped the screen. It was James.

James: "Just landed."

Corey: "That was quick."

James: "Flight only took fifty minutes. Tailwind."

Corey: "You waiting for a cab?"

James: "Yeah." Typing *"Miss you."*

Corey: "I miss you too."

James: "I want to kiss you again."

Corey: "Soon. Call me when you get settled tonight."

James: "Sexy video call?"

Corey: "So incorrigible."

James: "<winking emoji>"

Corey caught himself smirking. Kala was staring at him when he pulled himself away from the screen.

"Wow. You *really* like him."

"Probably a little too much."

"I thought James was straight."

"So did he."

"And his fiancé?"

"They split. James said he did everything he was supposed

to do. But it didn't work. Don't think he wanted it to. She broke it off with him when he became increasingly distant with her."

Kala frowned. "I don't know, Corey. I'm worried."

"He wants this … I know he does. You should have seen him this morning. Holding me—kissing me." Corey grinned. "Loving on me."

Kala crossed her arms. "When do you see him next? He lives in Victoria, doesn't he?"

"Next week. Winter Games. I'm going to spirit him away from his parents' watchful, religious eyes. Take him back to my room … and do very, very naughty things to him."

"He better not hurt you." Kala rose to her feet. "Okay, lover boy, I'm off. I'll be back next week. Tuesday, right?" She strolled over to the door and opened it.

"Yeah, Tuesday. Thanks again for looking after the boys."

"Anytime, bro."

And then she was gone. She had every right to be worried. He was worried. What if James arrived home and changed his mind? Decided he didn't want to continue with him after all.

Corey headed to his bedroom and flopped down on his bed. He rolled himself in a blanket and closed his eyes. James would call him later. He was sure of it.

Or was he?

Chapter Thirteen | James

The taxi wasn't nearly fast enough. James wanted to be home. Unpacked, messages to his parents returned. Relaxing. He wanted to be on a video call with Corey.

James leaned back and stared at the ceiling of the cab. He was filled to bursting. Filled with contentment. Filled with joy. His heart shouldn't feel this good. What he was doing—it was wrong. He knew that. But he didn't care. Being with Corey was all he cared about.

He sighed and grinned.

Every fiber running through his body wanted this. Every word, every touch—every scent. He wanted it all. He wanted to spend the rest of spring snowboarding with Corey. Cooking—laughing. Teasing—kissing. Wrapping Corey up in his arms.

Ravishing him.

And falling asleep together.

It had all happened so fast. One minute, snowboarding. The next, jerking Corey off and cumming on his back. He grinned. And the shower. He'd run his lips over every inch of Corey's skin. It had been glorious. Glorious and good. He knew in his soul it was good.

He clenched his fist.

His parents could never find out. He'd have to find some excuse to keep from dating any more women from the church. Even though his mother would be relentless. He tapped his finger on his leg. Maybe he could tell her he was too devastated by his breakup with Julie.

That excuse wouldn't last long. But it might stall things for a while.

The cab pulled up to his apartment building. He paid the cabbie, clambered out, and hauled his stuff to his apartment. It was dark and cold inside. His cat Patches had passed away three months ago, and he hadn't been able to bring himself to share his life with another cat yet.

He let everything drop onto the floor in the front entry. He looked at his phone. He needed to check in with his parents to let them know he was home safely. They'd be worried.

Two rings and his mom answered.

"How was your weekend, James?"

"Good. Really good. Snow was great."

"Good weather?"

"Perfect."

"You stayed out of trouble?"

"Nope." He grinned. "Went to a gay bar."

"James, please."

"Saw some drag queens."

His mom laughed at the other end of the line. "You're wicked teasing your mother like that."

James sighed. "I was perfectly respectable, Mom."

"Meet any girls?"

"Not ready." James scrubbed his face with one hand. "I'm tired, Mom."

"Yes, of course, son. Call me tomorrow."

"Will do. Love you."

"Love you too."

James tossed his phone on the dining room table. A quick bite to eat and then he'd call Corey. Food hadn't been on the menu today. They'd been too busy getting to *know* each other.

He yanked open the fridge. There was a sandwich that didn't look too suspicious. He'd only been away for three days. Caution to the wind. He took the sandwich and his phone with him into his bedroom. After changing into some sweats, he climbed onto the bed.

Ham and cheese sandwich eaten, he deposited the empty plate on his bedside table and called up Corey's number on his phone. He opened a video call and waited for Corey to answer.

Corey's smiling face filled the screen.

"Hello, you've reached Corey's sex line."

"If that's the case, I'm wearing too many clothes."

"I'll remove them the next time I see you."

"Deal." James leaned back against his headboard. "How are your dogs?"

"My dogs?" Corey made an attempt at looking shocked. "You want to know about my dogs? I'll have you know; I've had a grueling day. Rolling around under blankets, sweating—showering with a hot guy. The works. You not going to ask how I'm doing?"

James chuckled. "How are you doing?"

Corey touched the screen with his thumb. "Completely infatuated."

"I was thinking the same thing." James exhaled. "We're good, right?"

"Why wouldn't we be?"

"We're both home now. Back to real life. The weekend seems like a dream."

Corey blinked, long and slow at him. "The best dream I've ever had."

James sighed. "Good. Me too."

"You locked in for the Winter Games."

"I'll do that tomorrow and book my flight and hotel."

"I'll text you where I'm staying."

"Perfect." James yawned. "God … I'm tired. It's like I barely slept or something."

"Funny that. Phone me tomorrow night?"

"Will the sex line be open?" James winked at him.

"For you, tiger, of course."

"Then, yes. I can't wait. Have a good night."

"Goodnight."

James ended the call and let the phone drop on his bedding. He laughed and slapped his hands over his face. This relationship with Corey was the craziest thing he had ever done.

And damn, it felt good.

The veterinary office was busy. James had been running ever since he stepped through the doors at seven in the morning. Because he wasn't around as much as the other technicians, he was relegated to doing mundane jobs. Nail trims. Blood draws. Anal gland expression. Maybe, if he got lucky, a few IV catheters and radiographs. His latest customer was an elderly Shih Tzu with a temper. She needed a nail trim. He'd been forced to put a soft cat muzzle on her short nose to keep her from biting him and the other vet tech he was working with, Sharon.

"She's feisty," Sharon said.

"Every single time."

James couldn't help humming while he worked. It was impossible to stop thinking about Corey. Their weekend together and the video calls they'd been having every night.

A slow smile stretched across his face. A couple of those calls had turned into more than just talking. He was knocking down the walls of his church's teachings all over the place.

"You're chipper today," Sharon said. "Anything you want to share?"

James snorted out a laugh. Clip—clip. "Maybe."

"Oh … now you have to tell me."

James looked up at Sharon. He'd been subjected to the female vet techs sharing stories about their love lives for years. Maybe it was his turn.

"I met someone."

"Last weekend?"

"Yup. Up at Big White."

"A snowboarder?"

"Yeah. They love it. We did so many runs together. Cooking together, too."

"This someone have a name?"

James finished the last nail and removed the small dog's muzzle. He set the clippers down on the table and leaned in close to Sharon.

"It's a guy."

Sharon's eyes opened wide, and a smile spread across her face.

"Well, that *is* news. I didn't know you were bisexual."

James shook his head. "Don't think I am, to be honest."

"You think you might be gay?"

"Pretty sure." James smirked. "There were definitely *indications*."

"Oh … so a sexy weekend, was it?"

James hoisted the small dog into his arms. "I've never been so happy."

"Well then, I'm glad you met your special someone. Few people deserve it as much as you do. You're one of the sweetest people I know."

"Are you trying to coerce me into doing the next fecal

smear?"

Sharon spun to leave the room. "That's a distinct possibility."

Chapter Fourteen | Corey

It was a beautiful sunny day, but after a long flight to P.E.I., Corey was ready to find his hotel room and crash. James had managed to book into the same hotel as him. Different but adjoining rooms with his parents. They were crazy serious about keeping an eye on him.

Corey slid his key card into the lock of his hotel room, heard the click, and opened the door. The room was standard fare. Queen bed, bedside tables with lamps that were screwed to the surface. A chair and desk with the obligatory ice bucket and two paper-wrapped glasses.

He threw his luggage on the bed and headed for the bathroom. He'd been holding his bladder through the last part of the flight, squirming in the cab—and now he was near bursting. He hadn't dared to use the bathroom on the plane. He was deathly afraid of small spaces.

After getting the relief he needed, Corey flopped down on the bed and looked at his phone. No messages from James yet. He had hoped they would be on the same flight. Catch sight of each other. Corey desperately wanted to lay eyes on James in the flesh.

Corey: "I'm in my hotel room."

James: "Just landed. Be there soon. <heart emoji>"

Corey: "Can't wait. I'm in room 404."

James: "I'll drop off my luggage and tell my parents I'm going to see my coach."

Corey: "I'll be waiting."

James: "Naked, I hope."

Corey: "You really are incorrigible. Love it."

James: "I better go. My mom is getting suspicious of all my texting. Any minute now, she is going to start hovering over my shoulder to see who I'm talking to."

Corey: "She would do that?"

James: "It's bad. I'm going to have to delete this thread in case she takes my phone to see who I've been talking to."

Corey: "And you'd just let her?"

James: "I wouldn't disobey her. You wouldn't understand."

Corey: "<crying emoji> Okay. See you soon."

Corey set his phone on his chest after ending his texting session with James. It felt weird knowing James was going to delete everything they had just said to each other. To absolutely erase his existence. He couldn't wrap his head around it. He'd never been a religious type. Didn't even believe in God. James, though … came from deep within the church.

It made him nervous. James was taking a huge risk by being with him. The hanging out snowboarding was probably fine with James' parents. But he suspected that cooking together and sleeping on James' sofa might be considered too much. What they had done after that—all the sex. The fallout from that, if his parents found out, would be insane.

Corey closed his eyes. A quick nap until James arrived sounded like the best idea. He was competing tomorrow morning and needed to be well rested. A couple of hours with James was likely out of the question. James would never be able to get away with that. He'd be lucky to get half an hour with him. But it was more than he'd had all week. He needed to be held by James again. Kissed by him—devoured by him.

His cock thickened in his pants. Memories of what they had done together the week before played on repeat in his mind.

James' willingness to experience new things had been intense.

In the shower after soaping him up and rinsing him off, James had laid open-mouth kisses up and down his neck, across his collarbone, along the center of his chest—both nipples—sucking gently on them. Corey shifted on the bed. James: down his abs, across to each hipbone—then took his cock into his mouth. His method had been tentative but effective. He'd even swallowed.

Corey reached down and rubbed the front of his jeans. He was going to be *so* ready when James showed up. He sat up and stripped his shirt off over his head then pulled his shoes and socks off. His jeans zipper was next. He was going to do what James had asked—be naked.

Napping could wait for another time.

He slipped off the bed and headed to the bathroom. He had plans. Whether James would go for it was anyone's guess, but he was going to be ready. He'd brought the necessary supplies.

Cleaned and ready, a soft knock on the door could be heard. Corey peered through the peephole before opening the door. He pulled it open just enough for James to make his way into the room while hiding behind the door in his current state of complete undress.

James pushed the door closed, smirked at Corey, and wrapped his arms around him.

The first kiss was desperate, attacking each other like two men who had been without water for days. When they pulled away, they were both gasping.

Corey found himself emotional enough to shed a few tears.

"I missed you so much." James brushed his fingers through Corey's hair then ran his palm down Corey's cheek, stopping there to brush some tears off Corey's cheek with his thumb.

"I haven't been able to stop thinking about you."

"Me either." James perused Corey's body. "Man, you're gorgeous."

Corey absently stroked his cock. "You have too many clothes on."

"Easy fix." James threw his coat onto the back of the chair by the desk. He deftly removed the rest of his clothes, then dove onto Corey's mouth again. James clung to him, racing his hands up and down Corey's back—and onto his ass.

Corey pulled away, touched James' shoulders, and looked into his eyes.

"I want you inside me."

Corey could see the internal conflict happening in James' eyes. The tiger in him was game; the church boy—not so much.

James led Corey over to the bed and turned back the covers. It was cold in the room. "I'll do anything for you," he said. "For us. Anything for us."

Corey climbed into the bedding and James followed. Face to face and chest to chest, Corey slung his leg over James' hip and kissed him. Deep. Their hard cocks touched, and Corey undulated his hips to bring the contact closer. He'd been dreaming of this—renewing the intimate connection they had shared. There was something special happening between them.

"I want to make love to you," James whispered.

Corey sucked in a breath. This was so fast; the language James was using. But it felt right. Fast but true to where they were in this relationship. And it *was* a relationship. They had gone past this being a simple series of hookups. It was obvious that James felt the shift as deeply as he did. *He wants to make love to me.* Corey's heart was singing.

"I put some condoms and lube in the bedside table drawer over there." Corey pointed to the table he was referring to. "I didn't want to leave them on top and assume you'd be into it."

James kissed Corey then rolled over, opened the drawer, and retrieved the supplies. He examined them, flipping the condoms to see the front and back, looking at the label of the lube. These objects were foreign to James. Corey could see it on his face.

"Hand me a condom," Corey said. He took the package James handed him, ripped it open, and removed the condom. "I'll help you put it on if you like." He smiled at James.

"That would be a good idea." James lay back on his pillow as Corey rolled the condom onto his hard cock. James shut his eyes, moaning as Corey's hand stroked the condom into place.

"That felt way too good."

Corey smiled, picked up the lube, and reached for James' hand. "You can do this part." He poured a generous dollop of lube into James' hand.

"What do I do?" James asked, rubbing his fingers together, playing with the viscosity.

"Start with yourself. Coat the condom." Corey lay on his back and let his legs fall open. "After that, you'll figure it out."

James stroked his cock to cover it in lube, then positioned himself between Corey's legs. His hand moved slowly until he contacted Corey's skin. He lay his palm on the crease of Corey's ass, distributing some of the lube, then slipped his fingers past his flesh—touched Corey's hole.

Corey groaned and threw his head back against the pillow. *Fuck.* This was happening.

James slipped his pointer finger into Corey's hole and twisted it around, then plunged deep. He pumped it a couple of times. Only stopping when Corey grabbed his hand.

"That's enough. Save that for your cock."

James grunted, kissed Corey's knee, and wiped his hand on

the bedding.

"Do you need to roll over onto your knees?"

Corey touched James' arm. "You stay right there. I want to see your face."

The confusion that appeared on James' face was endearing.

"Trust me, it'll work fine," Corey said in response.

James crawled forward, placed one hand to the left of Corey's shoulder, and grabbed his cock with the other. Corey guided James until he was in position. A moment of hesitation clouded James' eyes. He leaned forward and kissed Corey.

"This is hard for me," James whispered. "It kind of solidifies things."

"You don't have to if you don't want to."

"I never said that." James smiled down at Corey. "I want to make you feel good." He pressed forward until his cock breached the ring of Corey's hole. He inched in until Corey gasped and shut his eyes. James stopped his advance. "Am I hurting you?"

"It's a good hurt … believe me." Corey placed his hand on James' ass and encouraged him to sink his cock deeper. "Fill me."

James descended fully. "Oh, man … that feels tight." He withdrew halfway and then rocked his hips forward, causing Corey to swear and dig his fingers into James' ass.

It was pure bliss having James' cock buried deep within him.

"Again, James."

James sunk into a rhythm of sorts. He was awkward and his cock often slipped out of Corey's ass, but Corey couldn't have been more captivated. The look on James' face was one of concentration and wonderment. His eyelashes fluttered and he kept licking his lips. He was panting above him; sweat falling in delicate drops on Corey's arms.

Corey touched James' face and brushed his thumb along James' bottom lip. He was getting close. Despite James' inexperience, he was hitting the right spot every few strokes.

He might be able to cum without touching himself.

James shifted his position.

Fucking hell ...

"Oh my god, James ... yes ..."

James had altered his angle, slipping back and forth smoothly over the spot that would get him there. Corey wanted James' mouth on his. He wrapped his hand around the back of James' head and pulled him to his lips. Tongues seeking each other out, Corey reached his climax.

Corey spilled free, coating his abs with each pulse. James sunk onto his haunches, grabbed Corey's thighs, and increased his pace. His attention was on the small pools of fluid on Corey's stomach—then on Corey's face. James closed his eyes, grunted, and came.

The look of blissful satisfaction on James' face had Corey's heart surging. James leaned forward and gave Corey a soft kiss. He climbed past Corey's thigh and laid down beside him. He rolled onto his side, slung his arm over Corey's waist, and tugged him close.

"I have a confession to make," James said.

"Is it something naughty?" Corey smirked.

James sighed. "No." He stroked the back of his fingers down Corey's cheek. "I think I might be falling for you."

Corey's mind nearly exploded. James Cartwright, the man he'd simply dreamed of kissing, had just expressed some serious feelings for him. He wasn't sure what to say. His own feelings were running so much faster. He was hooked—in love.

Truth time. He trusted James.

"I'm in deeper—I've totally fallen."

James blinked at him then his eyebrows rose. "You're in love with me?"

Corey pressed his lips together. He'd never spoken those words before. Every relationship he had ever been in had ended before any serious feelings developed. He had always preferred it that way. His heart had been closed off to avoid getting hurt. His dating life had been superficial—until James. James had broken through all sorts of barricades.

It happened so fast, his love for James. Likely because he had been in proximity to him for years. The hours and hours on the phone. They'd connected on a spiritual level.

"From my very soul," Corey answered.

"You're wreaking havoc on my heart." James kissed Corey. "I wouldn't have it any other way." He pressed his forehead against Corey's. "Horrible timing. I'm sorry … but I have to go."

"So soon?" Corey gripped James' shoulder.

"My mom will be expecting me back by now." James rolled away from Corey and left the bed. He stripped off the used condom, wandered across the room, dropped it in the garbage, and went in search of his clothes. They were scattered all over the floor, mixed with Corey's.

Corey joined him and slipped on his underwear. James, dressed, went to wash his hands, and then pulled on his coat, and headed for the door.

Corey followed him.

"When will I see you again?" Corey reluctantly opened the door.

"I'll try to escape again soon. Maybe tomorrow morning after Big Air."

Corey leaned against the doorframe as James stepped into the hallway. He sunk onto the lips offered him, tasting James, committing it to memory, the feeling of his mouth, and the desirous arms wrapped around him. He clung to James, not wanting to let him go.

"James?"

James jerked back and shoved Corey away from him. Corey regained his footing and peered down the hallway. A rigid, stern-looking woman with a horrified look on her face stared at them.

Shit.

Corey ducked back into the room. James' mom … it had to be. She had seen them kissing. Seen the desperation in the way they were gripping each other—the passion of their embrace.

James cleared his throat. "Mom. What are you doing here?"

"I got off on the wrong floor." She pointed in the direction of Corey's door. "The Lord's doing. Praise Jesus. He led me to witness this debauchery." She huffed through her nose, her eyes mere slits as her face contorted. "James, tell me this man led you astray. Coerced you. Tricked you."

"It's not what it looks like, Mom."

James' mom balled her hands into fists, squeezing them tight. "Lies."

"Please believe me." James walked toward his mother. "It was just one kiss. I *was* led astray. He doesn't mean anything to me."

Corey took a step back and gripped the doorframe. His eyes burned; tears pooled and rolled down his cheeks. To be simply denied was one thing. This … was agonizing. *He doesn't mean anything to me.* Those words from the same man who had moments before *made love* to him. The same man who had told him he was falling for him.

He slapped a hand over his mouth as James sunk to his knees in front of his mother.

James bowed his head. "I've sinned. Please forgive me."

"That's for the church to decide." She crossed her arms. "You're finished competing until you've prayed for forgiveness and begged for mercy from Christ. Pastor Jim will guide you."

James rose to his feet. "Yes, Mother."

Corey couldn't watch anymore. He shut the door.

Shutting and soothing his heart wouldn't be as easy.

Two rings and she picked up. His sister Kala knew he was supposed to be on the slopes early in the morning, competing. It was two in the morning. There was no reason he should be calling her.

"What happened?" she asked.

Corey was silent. The lump in his throat was stopping him from speaking.

"What did he do to you, Corey?"

"Dumped me," he managed.

"Geez, I knew this wasn't going to end well." Kala paused. "What happened?"

"The church sucked him back in."

"What do you mean?"

"His mom caught us kissing."

"And … what."

Corey sobbed aloud, coughing and sniffing. "He dropped to his knees in front of her. Said I meant nothing to him. That he had sinned … and asked for her forgiveness."

"Shit, Corey. That's fucked up."

"Kala, I had just told him I was in love with him." Corey shuddered through a breath. "He had just made love to me. Told me he was falling for me."

"I don't get it. All that and he just bailed because his mom caught you?"

"He kept telling me, I wouldn't understand … about his mom and the church."

"That was an understatement."

"I'm so lost, Kala. I thought we were going somewhere special with each other. That we had a future. That I had found my guy. The one I would spend forever with."

Kala's huff was audible through the phone. "I'm going to kill him."

"I appreciate you saying that. But leave it be."

"Just one phone call."

"No, Kala."

"All right. Take that away from me." Pause. "So, are you still planning to compete this week?"

Corey sighed. "I don't think my heart would be in it."

"You gonna come home?"

"Yeah … tomorrow morning if I can get a flight."

"I'll be waiting for you."

"Thanks, sis."

Corey ended the call, opened a travel app, and booked a flight. That should have been the end of it, but like a cruel twist of fate, James and his parents were on the same flight as him.

Sitting right behind him.

Shoving down his claustrophobia, Corey walked to the bathroom a couple of times during the flight, just so he could see James, and determine if it was truly over between them.

Every time he passed by him; James lowered his gaze, refusing to look at him.

It was over.

It was actually over.

Corey slumped down in his seat and looked at his phone.

Staring at nothing. He sensed James stand up behind me. The brief squeeze on his shoulder nearly made him cry.

James was still his.

There was hope.

Chapter Fifteen | James

James stared at his lap as Pastor Jim continued his prayer, asking Jesus to forgive the transgressions of one of his servants. James wiped his sweaty palms on his jeans. He'd been in the pastor's office for almost an hour. His parents sat behind him to observe and witness.

"Now, James." Pastor Jim took a seat in the chair behind his desk. "You need to confess all your sins in detail. It is the only way you will be granted forgiveness."

James furrowed his brow. "I kissed him. That's all."

The pastor leaned back in his chair and crossed his arms. "Your soul is in mortal danger here, James. You need to be honest. Confess each sin. Restore your salvation."

"Okay … okay." James gripped his knees. "He gave me a blowjob."

"And that's all?" The pastor asked. "Are you holding back?"

"Fine …" James sighed. "I jerked him off numerous times. Gave him a blowjob." He looked up at the pastor, the last remnant of his defiance surfacing. "Swallowed."

"Penetration?"

James' chest heaved. "Yes. I penetrated him."

The gasp from his mom filled the room. Her soft weeping trickled over his shoulder.

The pastor tapped his fingers on his desk. "Thank you, James. You've taken the first step. Now that you've unburdened yourself, and spoken your sins aloud, do you feel better?"

Sadly, he did.

"Yes."

"You need to make a phone call," the pastor said. "Phone this man and tell him it's over."

James nodded. "I will."

"Now, James," his mom said. She tapped James on the shoulder and handed him his phone. James closed his eyes. He knew it was the right thing to do, but it was going to hurt regardless.

He'd been falling in love with Corey.

Who was he kidding?

So much more than falling.

He would remember the time he spent with Corey forever. James selected Corey's number and turned on the speakerphone. Corey picked up after the first ring.

"James, what the hell? I've been phoning and texting you all week."

"My mom took my phone away."

"What the fuck, James?"

"You wouldn't understand."

"Yes, you've said that before. And I don't ... I don't understand. I told you I loved you. And I do, dammit. I fucking love you. I know that means something to you."

James looked at the pastor. He was waving his hand, indicating James tell Corey what he was meant to relay. James' stomach churned. He felt like he was going to vomit.

"Corey, look ... I can't see you anymore."

"What? Are you serious? You're going to listen to them? They're insane, you know that don't you? No better than a goddamned cult."

James sobbed and tucked his forehead into his palm. "Corey ... I can't ... I just can't." He could feel his heart ripping in two. He was never going to recover. No matter how many women his mother demanded he date, he was going to refuse. That much he could do to preserve his feelings for Corey. He would remain alone. A solitary life dreaming of Corey in his arms.

The tears began to flow in earnest. They laid down wide wet streaks on his cheeks.

"I love you too," he whispered. Corey needed to know that much at least. James ignored the shriek followed by sobbing that erupted from his mother as he spoke those words.

His father said nothing. They would most likely have a debrief later. His mother grabbed the phone away from him and ended the call.

James walked the pew, laying down a hymn book every few feet. This was part of his service to the church and his penance. Distributing and collecting hymn books, sweeping and washing floors; attending every single sermon for the past month. His life had become the church.

He moved to the next row. In each sermon, Pastor Jim made sure to mention that Brother James was struggling with the sin of homosexuality and that everyone should keep him in their prayers so his soul might be saved. He was made to stand so everyone knew who Brother James was. At first, it had embarrassed him. Now he was used to the stares and whispers.

Three times a week, he went to bible study. Deprogramming every day. *Praying the gay away*. He would arrive in Pastor Jim's office and spend the next hour on his knees begging God to remove the defect. Every day he walked away from that office as gay as the first day he had gone in there. There was no mistaking it now. God was determined to cause him pain.

He slumped down in a pew and pulled out his phone. His mother had changed his number and deleted Corey's. He hadn't memorized it. Even if he wanted to, it would be difficult to contact Corey. He leaned back and stared at the ceiling. He had tried to retain his memory of Corey's voice, but it was disappearing. If he concentrated, he could remember the taste and feel of his lips.

He still loved Corey, desperately. He knew that would never go away. He'd admitted as much to Pastor Jim. The pastor's answer had been that God would ease his pain over time. As long as he didn't act on his homosexual yearnings; that he remained chaste until marriage, all would be well.

James didn't believe him for a second.

As for marriage, his mother had tried to set him up with the few women who were willing to take on a project; to ignore his incurable homosexuality. He had outright refused. God had chosen not to remove his temptation. He'd never make a good husband for any woman.

And he'd made a promise to Corey in his mind. Corey was the only person he would ever love. His heart belonged to an incredible man. A beautiful, sexy, caring, funny …

James shuddered. A moan of agony escaped. He wanted to hold Corey again. Have him fall asleep on his chest. Kiss him—bring him pleasure. Laugh, snowboard … just be with him.

He turned his mind to happier times.

He smiled, remembering how Corey had insisted on flirting with him when they met up at that pub; Winter Pride. Joyous and free; Corey all smiles. The first stirrings of attraction. How quickly things had moved after that. They were like two puzzle pieces finding their match.

James sighed and rose to his feet. The church would be

filling soon.

The animal shelter was full. Dogs, cats, and a few bunnies. James was thankful his mother had let him keep his volunteer position in a place he loved. Caring for animals and placing them in their forever homes brought him some sense of peace.

James finished scrubbing the last of the dog kennel floors. It was a large concrete-slabbed room with ten chain-link fence kennels that had an opening to the outside. The dogs were all outside, enjoying the fresh air while he cleaned up the messes they had made.

He hosed off the industrial brooms and put them back in the closet. He rolled his eyes as he shoved them in there. *The closet.* He had certainly been shut firmly in one.

"You done?"

One of the other volunteers, Adam, smiled at him as he spoke.

"Yeah," James replied.

"Better you than me."

"It was my turn to put in the work."

Adam pursed his lips. "That's what he said."

James snorted. Adam was so obviously gay. It literally oozed out of him. To have that kind of freedom was an unattainable dream.

"He certainly did. Twice."

Adam smirked. "You trying to tell me something?"

"Nope." James walked the corridor between the line of kennels toward Adam. Last week, he had almost admitted to Adam that he'd briefly had a boyfriend. Except, that would have led to questions. Questions he didn't have the answers for. Questions he had been working to ignore.

The church was still his life. The daily prayers. The

pleading … the begging. It was exhausting. His parents could barely stand to look at him and his brothers had become distant. It was the closest thing to being shunned he had ever encountered. The last time his family had acted like this, his Uncle Tom had been forbidden to return to the church.

Rumor was, Uncle Tom had a male roommate and only one bedroom in his tiny apartment. James had considered contacting him, asking for advice.

James looked at Adam. Perhaps wisdom from someone his age might better answer a question that was burning in his mind.

"Question, Adam."

Adam threw a hand onto one hip. "Shoot."

"Have you had a lot of boyfriends?"

"Why? You looking?"

James sighed. "I'm serious."

Adam furrowed his brows. "A few. Maybe three serious relationships."

"I messed up a serious relationship recently."

"Pray—tell." Adam stepped closer.

James crossed his arms. He may as well tell Adam the truth. It was crucial information in asking what he wanted to know.

"It was with a guy."

"What?" Adam gripped James' shoulders and shook them. "Why didn't you tell me you were gay? I would have ramped up my flirting."

"Exactly why I didn't tell you."

"So, what … you want him back?"

"No." James shook his head. "That's not an option. I'm wondering how possible it would be to live without giving in to my homosexual urges."

"Why on earth would you want to do that?"

"I have my reasons." Bringing up the church wouldn't serve any useful purpose in this conversation. Adam wouldn't understand.

"You're nuts, but it wouldn't be any different than if you were straight."

"So … we don't want *it* more than straight people."

"Jeez, what the hell are you talking about?"

The church had taught that homosexuality was a perversity. That homosexuals were sex craved. That they would have sex with anyone—anything.

"The guy I was with …" Color crept into James' cheeks. "I wanted sex all the time."

Adam shoved his shoulder. "That just means you liked him, you idiot."

Deep down, James knew Adam spoke the truth. He didn't feel like his attraction and love for Corey were perversions. It had been so damned good. As pure as what he had expected.

"Thanks, Adam. I needed to hear that."

"Anytime."

James headed to the desk to start working on some adoption applications. His heart felt better knowing he and Corey hadn't been any different than a straight couple. That their attraction and sexual desire hadn't strayed from what the church might think was the norm.

It brought him some solace.

Chapter Sixteen | Corey

Corey raised his head when he heard a customer approach the till. He'd been resting it on his crossed arms on the counter. Depressed didn't begin to cover how he'd been feeling for the past month. James had done a number on him. He'd even lost his passion for snowboarding.

And this job … damn, he wished he could quit. He wanted to be left alone, tucked up with a blanket in his living room. Just him and the glow of the television.

He went through the motions of greeting the customer. Saying, "Hello, how are you today?" *Who bloody cares?* "Did you find everything you were looking for?" *Like I give a shit.* He rang up the mountain bike, took the payment, and added the obligatory, "Have a nice day."

As soon as the customer left, Corey resumed his position on the counter. His boss wasn't in today, so there was no need to race around doing busy work. Everything looked fine. Yesterday, he restocked some of the smaller items. Dusting wasn't on his radar.

Corey groaned and shut his eyes. His love for James hadn't subsided even a little bit. His anger had. He'd been furious at James for shoving his love aside. His love—James' love for him. James had professed as much on the phone; that he loved him too.

Didn't matter. James had walked out of his life.

Still, like an idiot, amid a recurring breakdown, he had tried to call James—a message informed him the number was no longer in service. Riding on that low, he had called his coach and told him he was done snowboarding. He wouldn't be going into another season.

Corey wasn't even sure he meant it. His emotions were all over the place. His memories of snowboarding with James were the memories he wanted to be left with. Making new ones would be too painful. Seeing James in competition worse. Agony.

Sheer fucking agony.

His sister, Kala, was worried about him. She had been hovering. Dropping in, bringing food, and offering to watch the dogs for a few days if he wanted to get away. She meant well.

James had broken his heart. The last thing he needed was time away from Syd and Gus. His dogs knew something was wrong and had been smothering him with love.

Corey looked at his phone. It was almost closing time. He skirted around the counter and locked the front door. A few minutes early but no one was looking. His boss didn't make a habit of watching the security tapes. Corey wasn't even sure the cameras still worked.

He flicked off the lights and headed out the back door. After locking up, he slid into his car and slammed the door. The silence was glorious.

He burst into tears. When they were together, he'd gone as far as fantasizing about marrying James someday. Marriage—kids. His imagination had run away on him. Hearing that James loved him had torn a hole in his heart. One that could never be mended.

The life that could have been theirs—destroyed.

Corey wiped the tears from his face, sobbing. He was a mess. His life was a mess. Love had come on quickly with

James. Something he promised himself he would never do again.

He shook his head. *Who was he kidding?* He'd never find love like that again. He had no desire to try again. James had wrecked any chance of him starting a life with anyone. His trust in James had been broken. A level of trust that Corey had no intention of ever giving anyone else.

The car engine rumbled to life as Corey turned the key. He would go home. Order some food and park himself in front of the television. Completely ignore the movie that was playing, work his way through a box of tissue, and fall asleep on the sofa.

That was his life now.

Chapter Seventeen | James

James wasn't sure how he had ended up there. Flashing lights—loud music. Men. It was a beautiful summer night; warm with a light breeze, and he had been out for an evening walk in downtown Victoria. His feet and subconscious had taken over. The environment he found himself in had him breathing a sigh of relief. He felt at home here.

He took a seat at the bar and ordered a gin and tonic. As he sipped it, he reminisced about the night he and Corey had matched each other, drink for drink. Gin and tonics—shots.

The fireplace at his suite.

The feel of Corey's lips on his for the first time.

He spun the glass on the counter and looked around. Pride flags were draped from post to post. It had been an environment like this where he first realized he was attracted to Corey. That he wanted more from Corey. That he yearned for an intimate connection beyond friendship.

And they'd gone there.

God ... had they ever gone there.

James drained his glass. He'd never been in a true gay bar before. He knew they existed in the city. Knew where they were. There were two along the same street in the heart of the city.

He had wandered into the more salacious of the two.

"Can I buy you a drink? You seem to have run dry."

James looked over his shoulder at an Adonis of a man. Perfect face. Perfect hair—perfect body. James perused him up and down. The guy was dressed for attention. Black leather shorts hugged his crotch. A mesh crop top offered glimpses of his pecs. Then James met his eyes.

They were blue—like Corey's.

"Thank you, but no."

"You not here alone?"

"Alone—but not looking for anything."

"Then maybe next time, keep your eyes off the menu unless you want to order."

James rolled his eyes.

Whatever.

He turned back to face the bar and ordered another drink. His parents were expecting him for dinner, but he had a sudden urge to drink himself under the table instead. He was among his people. *Yes, his people.* He'd come to that conclusion when Pastor Jim's efforts to rid him of his homosexual temptations had failed miserably. He was gay. There was no denying it.

He looked at his phone. His coach had tracked down Corey's phone number for him. He had been too scared to phone it. Four months had passed since his mother caught them. Corey might have found someone else. He couldn't bear to hear those words from Corey.

He stared into his drink when a woman pointed at him, followed by the group she was with whispering amongst themselves. He'd been recognized. His face had been all over the sports news channels when he packed in snowboarding suddenly. Both he and Corey. He still couldn't believe Corey had stopped competing. He wished he could talk to him about it.

To hear his voice again …

James threw back his drink. If he didn't stop his thoughts, he'd start crying again. He paid his tab, slid off the barstool, and headed for the door.

"James?"

No ... stop it.

He was hearing things. The thundering music had him hearing things. He surged toward the door just wanting to get the hell out of there. He strode off down the sidewalk, the sound of Corey's voice ringing in his ears. If he hurried, he could still make dinner at his parents' house.

"James."

Slap-slap-slap; someone running down the sidewalk behind him. James increased his pace. He knew in his heart it *was* Corey. He didn't want to face him.

"James, stop!"

James took one long, slow step and stopped.

Just one look.

He turned and wiped a single tear from his cheek; the first of many threatening to spill. Corey stood right there before him. He backed up as Corey walked toward him.

This was going to hurt too much.

"Don't ..." Corey reached for him. "James, please. Can we just walk—talk?"

The best James could do was nod *yes*.

Corey fell in beside James as he turned and started walking. James wasn't sure where he was going now. Home had been his original destination. Home. Truck. Parents.

"You quit competing." Corey was the first to speak.

"I was too busy." James looked at the pavement. "The church had me too busy."

"Penance for your sins."

James stopped walking and stared at Corey. "It's not funny, Corey. What we did was wrong."

Corey grabbed James' arm. "You actually believe that?"

James looked down at where Corey's hand gripped his wrist, praying he would release it. The feel of Corey's warm skin on his brought back too many memories.

"I don't have a choice in what I believe."

"You always have a choice."

"Corey, stop. You don't get it."

Corey snatched his hand back. "Then what were you doing in a gay bar?"

James scrubbed a hand across his face. Corey was digging for something. And he was sure he knew what. "What's your point?"

"Good little church boys don't frequent homosexual establishments, do they?"

"I was walking. It was a mistake."

"What … you just randomly wandered in there?"

"Something like that."

Corey crossed his arms. "Bullshit."

James erupted. "What do you want me to say? That I'm gay?" He pitched his hands into the air. "Fine … I'm gay. Satisfied?"

"Satisfied? Not the least bit since the guy I loved more than life itself dumped me. Not satisfied for one goddamned minute." Corey spun on his heel and headed back toward the bar.

Corey's anguished retort tore a new hole in James' heart. His love for Corey still burned hot—like fiery everlasting embers in his soul. He wanted to run after him.

And then what?

Anything—absolutely anything to be near him—that's what.

"Corey, wait."

He didn't care what came next. He just knew he wanted it

to be with Corey.

Corey stopped and turned. He was crying.

"What, James ... what?"

"I just ... I want ..." James knew he looked and sounded lost. He was lost. Four months of church therapy were being torn down in an instant. He crumpled to his knees. "Please."

He no longer cared if it was a sin. His heart was aching and only Corey could bring him any peace. What they'd had was good—so good. So much love. How could God object?

"Please, Corey. I need you," he whispered.

Corey wiped the heel of his hand across his wet cheek, his lips parted. There was hesitation in Corey's eyes. James felt his desire to live spiraling into the depths.

The silence was excruciating, hanging fragile in the air.

Please ...

A sigh escaped Corey's lips. "I swear to God, James ... if you hurt me again."

James crumpled into a ball on the pavement, gasping for breath. He was sure his heart had stopped, waiting for Corey to respond. "I won't. I won't," he murmured into his clenched fist.

Corey squatted beside James and lay his hand on James' back. "We take this slow. The first sign you're thinking of bolting, I'm going to beat you to it. Deal?"

James looked up at him. "Anything. I'll do anything."

"For *us* ... I've heard that before." Corey helped James to his feet. "Where do we go from here? I'm only in town for a few days." Corey heaved out a sigh. "It's going to take me a while to trust you again, you do understand that. We're not going to jump right back in where we left off."

Yes, anything.

James couldn't take his eyes off Corey. The man was as

beautiful as he remembered. "How about a date? Like a real date. We've never had one of those."

"Okay." Corey looked pleased by the idea. "Where are you taking me?"

"Fins." Corey had told him how much he loved seafood. The romantic restaurant by the water was the perfect place to have their first date. "Tomorrow night … seven. I'll make a reservation."

"I'll meet you there."

There was an awkward pause. Then Corey turned and walked away. James wanted to run after him, take him in his arms, and kiss him. Fill his senses. Immerse himself in the intimate emotion they had once shared. The love between them was still beating strong, he could feel it, but he knew better than to follow through with his impulse. Corey had spoken the truth.

Trust was going to take time.

James looked at his phone. It was fifteen minutes past seven. Corey was late. Or maybe he wasn't coming at all. James stuffed the phone back in his pocket. He had Corey's phone number, but he didn't want to text Corey in case he *had* changed his mind. Why dig the knife deeper by having the man he loved explain the exact reasons he hadn't shown.

He looked up to see Corey jogging down the sidewalk toward him. "Sorry, I'm late." Corey arrived, winded. "Napping. Didn't hear my alarm."

"You're here now." It was a sedate answer. A completely different response was happening on the inside. His heart hammered away; thrilled Corey had kept their date.

"Shall we go in?" Corey pulled open the door.

James had requested a quiet table so they could talk. He

was pleased when the hostess sat them at the back of the restaurant in a corner without much risk of traffic. The building was a converted factory from the late 1800s. Wooden floors and beams. Low lighting. It was perfect.

"Shall we order a bottle of wine?" James looked at the menu.

"I'm good with a glass."

James nodded. Of course, Corey was going to play it safe. Avoid getting drunk. There was tension between them. He couldn't help but notice, Corey couldn't take his eyes off him.

"So, you quit competing too ... why?" James asked.

Corey leaned back in his chair and crossed his arms. "Why do you think? Depression is a real thing when two people in love are torn apart by religious fanatics."

James scowled. "They're not fanatics."

Corey shoved his chair back. "This isn't going to work."

"Wait." James reached across the table in time to grab Corey's hand. The connection sent tingles straight up James' arm. "I'll leave the church. If that's what it takes ... I'll do it."

James released Corey's hand.

Corey stared at him, then pulled his chair back to the table. "You'd do that?"

"Dammit, Corey ... of course I would. Last night, I realized something. The church means nothing to me if I can't be with you. I love you more than my salvation. You need to know that." Tears rimmed James' lower lids. "I wanted to call you. To reconnect. But I was too scared to find you. Afraid you'd moved on—afraid you'd fallen in love with someone else."

Corey leaned forward against the table.

"I could never love another, James."

James' heart jumped like a wild beast in his chest. His breath caught, paralyzed by the intensity of his emotions. It was true. Corey still loved him.

Corey settled back in his chair. "Let's order."

"Yes." James blinked to clear the tears and swiped the back of his hand across his damp cheek. "The mussels are great here. Lots of garlic."

"Sounds good."

"Order extra bread. Lots of deliciousness to sop up."

"Noted. I'll do that." Corey set his menu down. "What are you having?"

"The wild pacific salmon."

"Yum."

James looked up at Corey. Corey was grinning at him. "I remember the last time *you* said "Yum". We were in the shower together," Corey added.

James smiled. "And I was right … you were delicious."

They were interrupted by their server—John. The men placed their drink and food orders. Their glasses of wine arrived shortly after.

Corey lifted his glass over the center of the table. "To what might be."

James tapped his glass to Corey's. "To the possibility of love conquering all."

Corey looked unsure—his acceptance of the ardent sentiment reserved. James didn't blame him for feeling less than optimistic. He had a terrible track record.

They took a sip of their wine and placed their glasses on the table in unison. Corey caught James' gaze and winked at him.

There was still a chance.

Time passed with light conversation, telling glances, and smiles. Their love for one another was profound. Profound but fragile. James knew if he let Corey down again, there would be no going back to this. Corey had enough respect for himself that he would end it.

Their food arrived and Corey dug into his mussels with a zeal that matched his appetite for life. Corey was genuine in the way he presented himself. How James had deliberately hurt the man before him was beyond his comprehension.

The church had led him astray. Not Corey.

James played with the salmon on his plate, taking only a few bites. He was so apprehensive, he wasn't hungry. He couldn't slip up with Corey, or Corey would walk out of his life forever.

"You were right," Corey said. "This is amazing." He dunked a torn piece of bread into the bowl of empty mussel shells. Devising a better plan, Corey lifted and drained the shells and placed them in the little bucket the server had provided.

He reached across the table with a chunk of bread in hand. "Do you want some?"

James smiled. Dinner was going better than expected. He took the bread and dipped it into the melted garlic butter and wine the mussels had been cooked in. Corey grinned at him in anticipation of James having a taste of what he obviously considered orgasmic.

It was good—really good. The fact it had come from Corey's plate, was even better. It meant Corey was feeling comfortable with him.

James huffed out a laugh as the fluid ran down his chin. He barely caught it with his napkin before it descended to his neck. Corey snorted, laughing, watching the scene unfold.

They were good. This felt good.

James insisted on paying the bill. Once they found themselves outside, the ease between them lost its momentum. The date was over. James could feel it. They'd be parting ways now.

"Well … I'm this way." Corey jerked his thumb over his shoulder. The opposite direction of where James was headed. "I had a nice time, James."

James watched Corey's eyes, searching for evidence that Corey's trust in him was shifting. "Me too." He stared at the ground, his anxiety surfacing. "Are you doing anything tomorrow?"

"I'm busy with friends all day tomorrow. Starting with breakfast at The Rebecca."

"Oh …" It was a crushing blow. James only had a couple of days to convince Corey he was worth a second chance. He didn't want Corey to head back to Kelowna without a promise to keep in touch—a promise that Corey was committed to rebuilding their relationship.

"I can see you the day after. Maybe we could go for a hike."

James lifted his gaze. There was anticipation brightening Corey's face.

"Should I pick you up?"

"Yeah. I'm at the Cozy Suites on Johnson. Ten? A hike. Then we could go for lunch."

"I know the perfect place. It's all wilderness but there's a great restaurant nearby."

Corey smiled. "Can't wait."

An awkward silence followed. James broke it.

"Okay … bye. See you soon."

"Bye."

Then Corey turned and headed back to his hotel.

And James wandered off toward home.

Alone.

Chapter Eighteen | Corey

Dinner hadn't been as awkward as Corey assumed it might be. There was still an ease between them. Corey flopped down on the bed. James' proclamation that he would leave the church for him had shocked him. Saying he would and doing it were two different things, though.

He wouldn't push him on it. If James was going to figure out his values and desires didn't match what the church was telling him, and act on it, he'd do it in his own time.

Corey looked around his empty hotel suite. It would be nice to have James filling some of that empty space—to be back in James' arms. But he was going to take this slow. He couldn't bear to have his heart trampled on again. If James couldn't build that trust with him—it was over.

He flicked on the television. There was little possibility he would find a gay rom-com on the few channels available to him. He'd have to settle for a straight romance story. But that's what he needed right now. Some hope that love could prevail over adversity. He settled on a movie he'd seen before. His phone buzzed. It was a number he didn't recognize.

"I had a really good time."

Must be James.

Corey: "So did I."

James: "I'm going to miss you tomorrow."

James was taking some chances.

Corey: "You'll survive."

James: "I wanted to hold you before we parted ways."

Yup. He was being bold.

Corey: "Maybe next time."

James: "I'll cling to that."

Incorrigible.

Corey: "Goodnight, James."

A long pause.

James: "I'll dream about you tonight. Of you being in my arms."

Jeez, James.

Corey: "Please don't do this. Not yet."

James: "I can't stop thinking about you."

Corey: "You're on my mind, too."

James: "I'm desperately in love with you."

Fuck.

Corey: "We can't do this right now. Please."

James: "I'm sorry. Goodnight."

Corey flipped his phone over on the bed. It didn't buzz again. He couldn't concentrate on the movie and sleep didn't come easy. His mind was filled with James' words. *Desperately in love.* Corey felt as desperate as James did. Limiting their desire to express their love for one another was going to be painful. But the trust wasn't there yet. He simply didn't trust James with his heart.

The morning sun streamed through the draperies. Corey felt like he hadn't slept at all. He looked at his phone. He still had an hour before he had to meet his friends at The Rebecca downstairs.

Apparently, they had some of the best waffles in town.

He grunted at his stupidity, but he couldn't stop himself.

Corey: "Good morning."

A few seconds passed.

James: "Not really. I couldn't sleep. I kept thinking about you."

Corey: "Same."

James: "I want to hold you."

Corey: "James. I can't. Not yet."

James: "I understand."

Corey stared up at the ceiling.

Dammit.

Corey: "I can ditch my friends after breakfast."

James: "Are you sure?"

Corey: "I want to see you."

James: "Are you still up for a hike?"

Corey: "Pick me up at eleven?"

James: "Eleven. I'll be there."

Corey closed his eyes. This was insane. His friends were going to give him hell for this move. But a whole day without seeing James, when he was so close, was inconceivable.

He was down on the sidewalk outside the hotel ten minutes early. Breakfast had lived up to expectations. Their caramelized banana waffles with whipped cream had been unbelievable. He needed this hike to work off the number of calories he had consumed.

He fidgeted with his shirt. He was nervous. This was their second date. If he had just met James, there would be certain expectations after a second date. That had been his experience anyway. *Not this time.* His body was craving James' touch, but his mind knew better.

James pulled up in a white pickup truck. He smiled at Corey through the truck window and Corey just about melted onto the pavement. Joy—pure joy lit up James' face.

He climbed into the truck and fastened his seat belt.

"Where are we headed?"

"Witty's Lagoon."

"Perfect. Sounds watery. I love the ocean."

"Lots of that. It's an easy trip down to it. It's the hike back that's more of a challenge."

"I'm ready for it."

Corey stared out the window in silence as James drove. James had said it would take them about thirty minutes to get there. Most of the scenery was strictly highway. It wasn't until the last ten minutes that they turned into an area abundant with trees. After a couple of curves, James pulled into a parking lot. There were a few other cars there. Not many.

Corey wasn't sure why they hadn't spoken the entire trip. Conversation had come easily for them in the past. The laughing—the teasing. Last night had been awkward but good. The conversation had flowed at least. But now … maybe they were destined for failure.

He leaped out of the truck. James was right, the trip down to the lagoon was easy. Once they stepped out of the forest, the ocean was calm; its vastness stretched out from the wet, sandy beach. The sand was etched with rippling ridges, the result of the ocean's tide. Surrounding the beach; arbutus, cedar, and spruce trees. It was the perfect backdrop to spend some time together.

They found a log to sit on and enjoy the breezes coming off the water, cooling their sun-warmed skin. The summer had been a hot one.

Corey sat close to James, so their shoulders and bare thighs touched. It reminded him of their first trip up the ski lift together. James had been incredibly uncomfortable. Now James leaned back against him, closing any gaps, disregarding the heat of the day.

Seven words, a question, clawed at Corey's throat. They

hadn't spoken in the truck or the whole way down the trail other than the occasional, "Be careful of that root.".

He set his hand on James' knee.

"Are we going to be all right?"

James peered at him. "Honestly, I'm terrified to say the wrong thing."

Corey nodded. "Yeah, me too."

"I want this more than my next breath, Corey. For us to be together again."

"I want that too." Corey rested his head on James' shoulder. "I just don't know how to get there." He sighed. "God, I miss what we had."

"I'm so sorry." James turned and kissed Corey's head. "I fucked up. I let us down."

Corey pulled away. "You did more than that … you destroyed my entire world."

"And I'll never forgive myself for that." James didn't look away. "What can I do to make you believe in me again?" He jerked away and dug around his pocket. "Wait."

Corey furrowed his brow. "What are you doing?"

James pulled out his phone. "I have a call to make."

"Now?"

James held the phone to his ear after selecting a number. He cleared his throat. "Pastor Jim? Hey, it's James." James nodded. "I'm great. Never better."

Corey gripped James' arm.

Was he doing it?

"I'm down at Witty's Lagoon."

Corey's breath caught in his chest.

He was. James was doing it.

"Yes, it's beautiful." James cleared his throat again. "And I'm here with Corey." He exhaled as he listened to the voice at the other end of the line. "No, I won't be doing that."

Corey pressed his forehead to James' shoulder and closed his eyes. He waited for the words that would make all the difference.

"No. I'm telling you no. No more. I'm gay and I'm in love with Corey."

There it was. *I'm in love.* James was choosing their love over the church.

"Yes, I'm sure my parents will be very upset. That's their choice. I'm choosing love because that is what Christ taught. I won't be coming back to your church."

Corey's heart shifted. Life without James was a life not worth living. The trust wasn't built back entirely yet, but James had taken a significant step. They had a chance at forever.

Pastor Jim was still talking when James ended the call.

Corey released James' arm. "I can't believe you did that."

"I was serious when I said I would do anything to have you back in my arms."

Chapter Nineteen | James

It felt insane and uncomfortable. It really did. But there was also relief there, draping his mind in a sense of calm. And love—so much love. Breaking from the church was the right thing to do. It's what his heart wanted to do. His mind was struggling. His heart was not.

James hugged Corey to him. It felt good to be at his side. To have Corey clinging to him. He vowed to make every moment with Corey special. To show him how much he loved him. There would be no going back to the church—away from Corey. He was done with the homophobic rhetoric. The outright hatred and fear toward people he now considered kindred folk.

"Let's go for lunch," Corey said.

James smirked. "I can't believe you're hungry already. Did you have the waffles?"

"I certainly did. Absolutely gorgeous."

James hugged Corey even closer. "Kind of like you."

"Slow down, tiger." Corey rose to his feet and held out his hand to help James up. They headed toward the trailhead. This time, on the way back up the hill, they had lots to talk about. Their despair at not snowboarding anymore. Their jobs. James' volunteer work. Family.

Nearing the top of the trail, James discovered that even though Corey's parents were strict, they were also a bit goofy and very liberal. When Corey had *come out*, they had been very chill about it—accepting—loving. Corey even suggested that James should meet them sometime. It was more than James had been hoping for this early in their reconciliation.

"Do they live in Kelowna?" James asked.

"Vernon. Not too far away."

"Are you inviting me to come out to see you?"

Corey turned to look at James. "Maybe."

That was good enough for now. The fact Corey wanted to see him beyond the few days he was in Victoria was all the reassurance James needed to justify holding on to a bit of hope.

The men were winded by the time they reached the top of the hill and wandered into the parking lot. James slid in behind the driver's wheel and waited for Corey to buckle up before starting his truck. The restaurant he wanted to take Corey to was less than ten minutes away.

"On second thought," Corey started. "Let's skip lunch. I have something much better in mind."

The rapid thudding of James' exerted heart sped up even more. His mind began running amuck with possibilities. And by the tentative look Corey was giving him, he might be right.

Corey reached for James' hand. "Don't get any ideas. I'm not having sex with you. What I want is for you to hold me. I badly want to fall asleep in your arms." He squeezed James' hand. "Are you up for a nap back at my hotel?"

Anything.

Any glimmer of anything. James would take it.

"I would love to take a nap with you."

"Sweet." Corey smiled at James, then released his hand so James could drive. They fell into silence. He was nervous. Corey had to be too. This was a big deal. Cuddling held the potential of kissing and he'd been plagued by recurring dreams of tasting and feeling Corey's mouth on his again. Especially, the last two nights after running into Corey.

"What are you thinking about?" Corey asked as they pulled into downtown.

James looked over at him. "You. Always you."

A twitch of a smile pulled at Corey's cheek. "Please don't make me regret this."

"How?" James guided his truck into a parallel parking space. "What do you mean by that?"

"I just mean ... don't pressure me. This is just a nap."

"Jeez, Corey. I would never do that."

Corey nodded. "I know. I just wanted to make sure."

They climbed out of the truck and Corey led the way into the hotel. Corey linked his arm with James' as they rode the elevator. The need to have physical contact was strong for them both.

James tipped his head until it touched Corey's. They stood there and breathed in unison, side by side as the elevator ascended to the fourth floor.

The elevator door opened, and the moment was broken. Corey used his swipe card, and they entered his suite. It was warm. The summer sun had heated the room. Corey flicked on the air conditioning. "I just need to go to the bathroom," Corey said.

James looked around the room, then at the bed. He decided to stretch out on the tidy bedding while he waited for Corey to emerge. When Corey did, James could see by his expression, Corey was hesitating. James softened his voice, and whispered, "Come here ..."

Corey's chest heaved as he started at the end of the bed and crawled toward him. Slow and hesitant. James stretched out his arm for Corey to lie on. "I won't bite. I promise." Corey smiled and tucked himself in the crook of James' shoulder and lay his head against James' chest.

There was an audible sigh from Corey as he relaxed into James' embrace. He set his hand on James' stomach and stroked James' shirt with his fingertips. Small, delicate circles.

James tugged Corey in tight and kissed his forehead.

"I've been dreaming of this," he said.

"Me too. I've missed this more than anything else we did."

"Even the shower."

Corey chuckled against his chest. "That's a close second."

James licked his lips. The question needed to be asked. "Am I going to be allowed to kiss you?"

"I don't know yet."

Not the answer James was looking for, but he was willing to go at Corey's pace. It was all about building that trust back. Step by step, slowly, he was hopeful they would get back to the way they had been before. Not exactly the same, of course. A modified way of being together.

James closed his eyes. Having Corey in his arms was all he needed right now. Hearing him breathing beside him. Feeling the weight of him. Even his scent. It brought so much back.

He was more in love with Corey now than he had been before. Corey had impressed him. He respected Corey for standing up for himself—keeping his heart safe.

Corey turned and kissed James' chest.

And with that, they fell asleep. Exhausted by the exercise and the emotions that had been flowing between them; Corey setting down ground rules. And James' departure from the church.

When James awoke, Corey was lying in his arms, watching him. James couldn't help but smile. This was the way he wanted to wake up every day for the rest of his life.

"Good afternoon," he said.

"It is." Corey blinked and licked his lips. "You can kiss me

… if you want."

"Dammit, Corey … of course, I want." James cupped Corey's face and moved in. He covered Corey's mouth with his, their lips reacquainting themselves. They hummed in time with each other and deepened the kiss. James gripped the back of Corey's neck and Corey's hand went to James' shoulder, each tugging the other closer. It was like coming home.

James felt the shift when Corey decided they were veering into dangerous territory. He released Corey's mouth and stroked the hair away from Corey's forehead.

"That's going to keep me awake all night," James said.

"Ditto." Corey smiled. It made James' heart sing a song of absolute adoration.

"Can I see you again tomorrow?"

"My flight is tomorrow afternoon. I had to change it." Corey stroked his fingers along the stubble on James' chin. "It's at one. Maybe you could drive me … see me off."

James could feel his lungs deflate. They hadn't had enough time. He needed more time.

"Can you change your flight to the next day?"

Corey shook his head. "I have to get back to work. I only took a few days off."

There had to be a solution. James felt frantic. Their reconciliation could so easily go off the rails if they spent too much time away from each other.

"I need to see you again. Can I come to Kelowna?"

Corey was silent, studying James' eyes. "You can't stay at my place."

"No, I know. I'll get a hotel."

"I get Sunday and Mondays off. Can you manage something around that?"

"Just tell me when."

Corey smiled. "Pride is in two weeks. Going together might be a full-circle moment."

"That would be perfect." James stroked Corey's cheek. He wanted to kiss Corey again, but he wasn't going to make a single move unless Corey initiated it.

Corey touched James' bottom lip. "You are such a good kisser."

There was an invitation there. James extended his tongue and tickled the tip of Corey's finger then sucked it into his mouth. Their eyes met and time appeared to stop.

Corey groaned. "Fuck." He dragged in breath after breath, his shoulder rising and falling with the intensity. He pulled his finger free. "We need to stop."

James' fierce emotions as he stared into Corey's eyes had sent James into a trance. Breaking free from that was sudden and jarring. They had come far too close.

"I should go," he said.

Corey rolled away from James, out of his arms, and sat up. "Without question."

"Did I fuck up?" James sat up and set his hand on Corey's shoulder.

"No." Corey shook his head. "Not at all."

James released him and swung his legs off the bed. He was slow to rise. He didn't want to leave. Go back to his dark apartment. Away from the light he felt around Corey.

Then there were his parents.

He looked at his phone. He had muted it. Forty-six missed calls and a flood of text messages. The summary of the last text sent read that he was going to burn in hell.

So be it.

James wandered across the room. It would be best if he stopped by his parents' house on the way home. Take the verbal thrashing in person. It would set his resolve. That Corey was more important than everything else in his life. That he could no longer be dictated to—controlled.

"Everything all right?" Corey moved away from the bed, wrapped an arm around James' waist, and rested his head on James' shoulder.

"My parents are blowing up my phone." James held up his phone so Corey could read the latest text message from them.

"Yikes." Corey took the phone James' offered him and scrolled through the next few lines back in the text message. "Oh … James. I'm so sorry." He handed the phone back.

The line of text on the screen read, *"Return to Christ or never return to this family."*

James could feel his eyes welling up. His chest ached. He blinked. Tears streamed down his cheeks. He turned and hugged Corey to him, burying his face against Corey's neck.

How could they do this?

The sobs as he clung to Corey quaked his body—his soul. Corey held him tight. It was the comfort he needed. A huge part of his life was falling apart.

"God, James … are you sure?"

James pulled back, arms outstretched, clinging to Corey's shoulders.

"As sure as I've ever been about anything." James hauled in a shuddering breath. "My love for you means everything. If I have to walk away from them, that's what I'm going to do."

It seemed it was pointless discussing his decision further with his parents. They had made it quite clear what their stance was. They were willing to abandon their son for their beliefs.

"Fuck … James." Corey curled into James' arms, hugging James tighter than he had ever done before. The love flowing from Corey's embrace was debilitating in its ferocity. Fierce, powerful, and safe. He was safe in Corey's arms. Safe and loved.

"I love you," he whispered in Corey's ear.

"I never stopped."

Chapter Twenty | Corey

Corey never could have imagined how much James was willing to give up for him. How much he would give up for their love. His family. His whole damned family.

It made him feel guilty. How could he ask this much of the man he loved? To walk away from his entire life. To give up everything he had ever known.

"James." Corey squeezed James, then released him. He cupped James' face and gazed into his red-rimmed, swollen eyes. James' face was awash with tears. "Are you sure about this?"

"It's worse than I thought … they're disowning me." James broke eye contact and stared down at the floor. Maybe he was reconsidering. "I don't know …"

Corey stepped away. There it was. James was backpedaling.

James sat on the edge of the bed. "I don't know how they could do this to me." He looked up. "I fell in love … that's all I did. I found my person. My forever person."

Corey felt like he could breathe again. James wasn't denouncing him—declaring that everything they shared was evil. The man he loved was rightly stunned. That a family who had loved him his entire life would just ditch him. To declare their past meant nothing.

He felt his chest fill.

Those words James had spoken.

His forever person.

James had found his forever person. The confession sang in Corey's ears. Corey kneeled on the floor at James' feet, set his hands on James' knees, and waited for James to look at him.

"I'm going to ask again, James. Are you sure?"

Unwavering love flowed from James' beautiful brown eyes. "My heart is yours."

A piece of trust shifted back into place in Corey's heart. It was far from fully healed, but it was on its way to being mended. James had given up a lot for him.

He couldn't leave James like this. Distraught. Let him leave and go home. He rose to his feet. He climbed onto the bed, settled himself, his back resting against the headboard, and patted the spot beside him. "Come here … tiger."

James turned and stared at the empty space, made up his mind, and joined Corey. He tucked in close against Corey's side. He placed his hand in Corey's outstretched palm and clung to him as Corey closed his fingers around James' hand. They were in this together.

They sat like that for more than an hour. Corey didn't dare move. James had his hand in a vice grip. Every few minutes, he rolled through waves of tears. Devastated. James was absolutely devastated. Corey couldn't imagine his own family doing something like that. They had been so open and accepting of his sexuality when he had *come out*.

Eventually, James let out a long sigh and relaxed his grip on Corey's hand.

"You all right?" Corey ventured.

"Better."

It was getting late in the day. "I'm in the mood for pizza. How about you?"

James let out a soft laugh. "Yeah, I could eat."

"Movie?"

"I'd like that."

Corey passed James the television remote, then ordered a meat-lovers pizza. There was no reason to confirm with James about toppings. He was likely too numb to care.

As they waited for the pizza, they decided on a movie. They were thirty minutes into an action movie when the pizza arrived. Corey set the pizza box on the bed and handed James a napkin.

James was hungrier than Corey had anticipated. It was good to see him eat something. His world had just been torn apart. Losing his family would take an incredible amount of healing.

Time ticked on. Neither of them was paying attention to the movie. They kept glancing at each other between bites. Some pivotal words had been spoken today.

James' forever love.

Those words—their lives had significantly changed by having them spoken.

Corey wiped his fingers on the napkin and tossed it into the empty pizza box. They had some things to discuss. Corey was still hesitant about trusting James with his heart.

So damn close, though.

James shuffled down in the bed and closed his eyes.

Corey relaxed.

Tomorrow.

They could discuss it tomorrow. Corey curled up beside James and held him, his arm slung over James' waist, his face buried against James' neck. He was positive they lay there for hours before they fell asleep. Just content to be with each other—side by side.

Corey awoke to James weeping beside him; his sobs shaking the bed. It was pitch black in the room. He hugged

James to him.

"You're all right. I'm here," he whispered.

"How could they do that to me? Just dump me."

Corey stiffened. "Well … *you* did it to *me*."

James turned his head. "Don't ever forgive me for that."

"Don't be ridiculous." Corey pushed up onto one arm. "Someday. It'll come someday."

"I don't deserve forgiveness."

Corey leaned forward and kissed James' forehead. "Everyone deserves forgiveness."

"That's debatable."

"You know I love you, James. We'll keep at it—try to work this relationship out."

"I would be lost without you." James gripped Corey's arm. "Please don't leave me."

He wanted to reassure James. That he had no intention of leaving him. But he couldn't go there. Not yet. The best he could offer James—he would stay by him until it worked, or it didn't.

"I'm here now. That's what's important."

Corey was glad he couldn't see James' eyes. There would be so much sadness there. Not being able to speak the words James needed to hear, hurt.

He lay back down after James adjusted his arm so Corey could be enveloped by it. He was held tight to James' body, his bare feet brushing against James'. He settled his face on James' chest and breathed in the scent of him. A mixture of soap, sweat, and pizza.

It was oddly comforting.

He gripped James' shirt and fell asleep.

Corey stood inside the airport, staring out the window toward the tarmac, wishing he didn't have to leave. He and James had awoken entwined with each other. Tender kisses followed. Sighing and gasping, they had reaffirmed their devotion. James had been the first to pull away. Corey was grateful James had taken the initiative. Corey's conviction had been failing.

Any longer and he would have succumbed to desire. Stripped James of his clothes. Made love to him. Corey groaned. He missed their intimacy—their need for one another.

He stroked the handle of his carry-on luggage.

James had stayed the rest of the night, sleeping restlessly beside him. They'd had early brunch together, then James had driven him to the airport, and accompanied him inside. Waited with him in the check-in line. Walked him to the gate. Hung back until they lost sight of each other.

The hug goodbye had not been long enough. The kiss not deep enough. He longed for the man like he had done for none other. Love. That's what intense love felt like.

He almost turned around and ran for the door. Ran back to James. His gut clenched as he resisted the urge. He had a life to go back to. His sister, his dogs—his parents.

Now was not the time. He and James would have to figure out a way to knit their lives together. If they decided to stay together. If everything worked out.

Corey trudged along behind the line of people headed for the plane. He found his seat, threw his baggage in the overhead bin, and buckled in. It was only an hour's flight, but every second was going to take him further and further away from James.

He wasn't sure his heart could take it.

He had to hold on to the future. While in the hotel room, James booked his flight and hotel in Kelowna. To be there with Corey for the Pride Festival. It was only two weeks away and they had agreed to call each other every night. He gripped his armrest.

Maybe his heart would survive after all.

The dogs were overjoyed to see him back home. So was his sister. He had texted her the whole story on the cab ride home from the airport. She had been reserved in her responses.

James had hurt him horribly. She wasn't keen to see it repeated.

Corey lay on his bed and let the dogs climb all over him. They eventually calmed down and found places to curl up, ensuring some part of their bodies made contact with Corey's. They weren't going to risk having him leave again. It was the comfort Corey needed.

His trust in James was growing but there was a tiny spot in his heart that was scared. Downright petrified of being hurt again. They had spent less than forty-eight hours together. It was too soon. Too soon to put his heart on the line. Too soon to be thinking about their long-term future. Kala had reminded him of that—that it was going to take time.

They had two weeks before they saw each other again. Two weeks of talking. Two weeks without physical contact clouding his judgment.

His phone buzzed.

James: "You home?"

Corey: "Just got in. Dogs went crazy."

James: "They do tend to do that. I miss having a pet."

Corey: "Why don't you get another cat?"

James: "I might."

Corey: "Have your parents said anything else?"

James: "No. I tried calling but they're not picking up."

Corey: "Do you think they'll ever come around?"

James: "Not likely. My brother, Michael, reached out,

though."

Corey: "Wow, that's something at least. What did he say?"

James: "Not as harsh as my parents. He isn't planning on writing me off. He doesn't understand my 'affliction' as he called it, but at least he wants to understand."

Corey: "Well, that's great news."

James: "Even told me he loved me. The way I am."

Corey teared up. It was just so unexpected. Before he came out to his family, James had been incredibly close with his brothers. Corey had assumed those ties would be broken forever.

Corey: "I'm so happy for you."

James: "It was surprising." Pause. *"How's your sister taking it? Us."*

Corey: "She's skeptical. She doesn't trust you."

James: "That makes two of you."

Corey: "James, I'm getting there. I really am."

James: "Don't rush it. I want you to be sure."

Corey: "I will be." Pause. *"I need to take the dogs out."*

James: "That's one of the nice things about cats. They don't need a chaperone to do their business."

Corey: "Yeah, but you have that dirty box to clean. I prefer dogs."

James: "Well, you better get to it. We'll talk tomorrow?"

Corey: "I'll call you after work. We close at eight."

James: I'll be waiting."

Corey: "Miss you."

James: "Miss you too."

Corey rolled off the bed and called the dogs out into the living room. Their leashes were hanging in the kitchen by the door. The apartment was small with all three of them there. The dogs needed to go out regularly to get some exercise. They were happy, though. Happy and loved. He had adopted them from a shelter like the one James volunteered at. Brothers— abandoned when they got too rambunctious for their previous owner. They were certainly a handful.

As was his love life.

Chapter Twenty-One | James

James closed the texting app on his phone. Corey had said he was getting there—with his trust. Two weeks away from him was going to be hard. Being curled up in bed with Corey had comforted him. He felt safe when he was with Corey. Like the rest of the world was on hold.

He wrapped his arms around his body.

God. My parents. My family.

Away from Corey, they were on his mind again. His younger brother, Michael, might be willing to give him a chance but he was convinced his parents and his older brother, Matthew, never would. All his memories of the times they'd had fun as a family, their closeness—it was all tainted. Every Christmas, every school recital, every birthday … every snowboarding trip.

He found himself slipping on his boots and heading for the door. Tonight was the night he would normally go to his parents' house for dinner.

He was going to keep that date.

He was going to torture himself with their rejection. Remind himself of what he had done to Corey. How he had shoved Corey aside like he was nothing.

James pulled his truck into their driveway. His heart was frantic, rapid strikes thundering in his ears. He approached the front door. Michael pulled it open.

"What are you doing here?" Michael asked, keeping the door only partially open. He was hiding James' presence from those in the house. He must have heard James pull up.

"I need to hear it from them."

"No … no, you don't." Michael slipped out and closed the door behind himself. "Don't do this. Why would you want to do that to yourself?"

"I deserve it. I deserve the loathing. What I did to Corey was unspeakable."

"James, I don't get it, I really don't, but you must love this Corey guy a lot to be willing to put yourself through what is waiting for you in there."

James' father pried open the door. "Michael, who is it?"

"James." Michael stepped aside, slipped past his dad, and went back into the house.

"You can't be here," James' father said. "You're not welcome here."

"Dad, please. I'm in love. Why is that so wrong?"

"It's a perversion. It's not love."

James' breath caught in his chest. He took a step back. "You believe that? That my love for another human being is wrong. That it's wrong that I want to spend the rest of my life with him. Marry him—have children with him. Grow old together."

The repulsion on James' father's face tore at James' heart.

"You're a hypocrite!" James shouted. "Christ taught love and acceptance, yet you have none for me. You need to take a close look at yourself. You, Mom, and Matthew."

James' father crossed his arms. "You need to go."

"So, that's it … twenty-eight years of my life, erased. I'm your son, Dad."

"No. I only have two sons."

Oh, fuck. That hurt.

James stumbled back, almost falling down the steps. He had hoped his dad might break. They had always been so close.

Instead, he was being disowned.

He threw his arms out, backhanding the air with both hands.

"You know what … good! I have someone who loves me without condition! I don't need you and your rhetoric! I don't need the church! I don't need Mom! I have everything I need in Corey!"

"Then you'll rot in hell with him."

His father turned on his heel, stepped inside the house, and shut the door.

James climbed back into his truck. He was too stunned to cry. Instead, anger bubbled up. His entire life had meant nothing to the people he loved. His family. What kind of people abandoned one of their children? Discarded the gift of a child. Someone they were meant to love.

He pulled out his phone and selected Corey's number.

"Hey, tiger."

Corey's voice immediately soothed him. The impulse to surge out of his truck and hammer on his parents' door to yell at his dad some more, dissipated.

"I did something stupid," James said.

"How stupid? You're not driving to Kelowna, are you?"

"Would that be so bad?"

"No … no, of course not—tell me what you did."

"I went over to my parents' house."

"Um … okay. Why?"

"Honestly. I wanted to feel the rejection in person."

"Again … why?"

"Because I'll never forgive myself for what I did to you."

"James—that's over. You made a mistake. I won't hold it against you forever."

"But you still do."

"Dammit, James. Yes, it's still there. What you did obliterated me. You know that."

James leaned forward until his forehead made contact with the steering wheel. He tried to breathe normally but his chest was tight. Forgiveness and trust. They had a long road to travel.

"I never stopped loving you," Corey said. "I should have. I should have hated you."

That would have been the end for James. If Corey had told him he hated him. It was bad enough being rejected by his family. To be hated by the man he loved.

The end—the absolute end.

"Instead, I'm crazy in love with you," Corey continued.

"Enough to give me another chance with you?"

"That's what we're doing, James. I opened my heart, letting you into my hotel room. And you were gentle with it. You cared for my heart with love."

"I will never hurt you again."

"You can't promise me that, but I'll carry that with me. I know you mean it."

James looked up at the house. "My mother is staring at me from behind the drapes. I should go before they call the police."

"They wouldn't do that, would they?"

"Who knows at this point."

"Call me again, if you need to. I stay up late."

"Thank you."

"Goodnight, James."

The call disconnected. James' world felt empty. He started up his truck and drove toward home. It comforted him, knowing he could call Corey if he needed to.

As for his family, it felt good to be given the opportunity to break free from judgment. A life without someone constantly breathing down his neck. Pushing their expectations on him.

A life with Corey instead. A life filled with joy.

On the way home, James decided to swing by the animal shelter. He could build his own family. One with Corey and a furry beast. There was a cat he had been considering for weeks. She was fifteen years old, blind in one eye, and needed constant veterinary care. She was destined to spend the rest of her life in the shelter. He knew he could give her a loving, forever home.

James unlocked the door, slipped into the shelter, and flicked on the lights. Florence would be in the cat room, likely sound asleep as the other younger cats played around her. James found her sleeping at the base of a cat tree. He nudged her until she opened her eyes.

"Hey, Flo." James ruffled her fur. "You're coming home with me."

He made sure to leave a note for the manager saying he had taken Florence home with him. She curled up on the passenger seat and didn't make a single sound. She was simply content. Always. He'd spent more than a few hours in the cat room cuddling with her. She had been surrendered by a family whose elderly parent had died, leaving Florence alone.

James still had the cat box and toys that his cat Patches had used and enjoyed. Even Patches' cat beds were scattered all over the apartment. Florence would fit right in.

It felt good, carrying her into the apartment. A piece of his life had been returned to him. Florence already adored him. It would be an easy transition to live with him.

He texted Corey.

James: "I brought a cat home."

Corey: "Sweet! That's awesome. Name?"

James: "Florence."

Corey: "Sounds sassy."

James: "More like sleepy. She's fifteen."

Corey: "She's found a good home."

James: "She's already claimed the sofa."

Corey: "Hug her for me."

James: "Will do. Thinking of you."

Corey: "You all right?"

James: "I'll survive. Ready for bed."

Corey: "Wish I was there with you."

James stared at the screen. That was unexpected.

James: "You'll have to be satisfied with hugging a pillow."

Corey: "Can't wait to be back in your arms."

James stroked Florence's head. He was going to take a chance.

James: "Love you."

Corey: "Love you too. Goodnight."

James: "Night."

James rolled into bed feeling better than he thought he would after such a rough encounter with his family. He had Corey and he had Florence. She curled up on the bed at his feet. He'd filled her cat box with litter and fed her a few treats. She was entirely enamored.

Life felt good. Two weeks and he'd be able to see Corey again. Michael likely wouldn't have a problem checking in on Florence while he was away. He could count on him.

It would have to be enough. This life. And it would. It would be enough. His world was taking him in a direction he wanted to go. Not the path of marriage and children with a woman he had no interest in. That would have been torture. And so unfair. To everyone.

Florence purred against his foot.

He closed his eyes, thinking of Corey and the life they had

ahead of them. The uncertainty only crept in around the corners. Whether Corey would ever trust him again.

There was love there—so much love.

He rolled over and fell asleep.

Chapter Twenty-Two | Corey

Corey waited patiently in the arrivals area. He and James had talked to each other on the phone until the very last minute before James boarded his plane. To say they were excited to see each other didn't even cover the emotions they were feeling. Two weeks. Every night, a video call. Texting constantly throughout the day. Every day. They had learned so much about each other.

Corey wrapped his arms around his middle to calm himself.

Countries and cities they'd visited, childhood stories, dating disasters, career woes, and animals they'd cared for—their favorite colors. They'd discussed so much about their lives down to the smallest detail. They'd shared their future dreams for themselves. And their secrets. Corey had learned James used to paint and assemble model planes. And that James had a blanket in his dresser drawer he'd had since birth.

Corey had told James about the buckets of wooden trains he'd had as a child and even shared that he liked to be tied up during sex. James had groaned his approval and threatened to show up with a suitcase full of ropes. Corey had teased he already had plenty.

Sexual innuendos often dropped into their conversations. They hadn't discussed whether it was on the table or not for this visit, sex. It was a possibility. Talking to James on the phone and being in his presence were two different things, though. Corey would need to judge in person if his trust in James was sufficient to take a risk like that.

The flight arrival and departure board showed James' plane had landed. Corey moved to the front of the crowd. He wanted to be the first thing James saw as he descended the short ramp.

The delay was agonizing.

After a few minutes—movement. People appeared, dragging suitcases, one after another. Corey strained to see through them. The anticipation was palpable. Corey's hands were sweating.

Then, there he was—the man he loved.

James rushed down the ramp. Halfway across the arrivals area, he dumped his suitcase on the floor and ran at Corey. The ferocity of James' assault knocked the breath out of Corey. Wrapped in James' arms, his encircling James' waist, neither of them wanted to let go. They squeezed and clung tight to one another until they were both breathless.

James released Corey and cupped his face with both hands and planted an aggressive kiss on Corey's lips. The temptation was there to deepen the kiss, but they were in public. It was best to save that until they were alone. As it was, people were staring.

Corey gripped James' shoulders and put a bit of pressure on them, indicating they should stop. The last thing they needed was to be harassed by a bunch of homophobes. This was going to be a pleasant visit. Filled with love and pride. And he was—proud. Judging by James' reaction to seeing him again; kissing him in public—James was well on the road to *coming out*.

"Oh, my god …" Corey slung his arm around James' waist as they walked out through the doors into the stifling heat. "I missed you so fucking much."

"I know. Me too. That was the longest two weeks of my life."

Corey hailed a cab parked along the curb to secure it. He

hadn't brought his car. It didn't have air conditioning and it was too bloody hot without it. A typical Okanagan summer. He was already sporting a significant tan and it was only late June. July and August were going to be killers.

"How was work today?" James asked.

"It dragged on something terrible."

"Thanks for jamming out early to pick me up. I was so excited to see you. The thought of waiting until tonight was causing me a crazy amount of grief."

"No worries. Todd at work was getting annoyed with me going on about you. Practically kicked me out of the store."

James wrapped the crook of his arm around Corey's neck, pulled him close, and kissed his head. The affection in that kiss radiated straight down Corey's neck to his heart.

"Same," James said. "The other vet techs were glad to get me out of there. I wouldn't stop talking about you."

"My sister has definitely heard enough."

"Is she feeling any better about us?"

"She has serious reservations. Once she meets you … she'll get it."

Corey slipped into the backseat of the cab while James told the driver the name of his hotel. They were sticking to the plan. Corey didn't want James to stay at his apartment. It would put too much pressure on them both to have sex. That remaining sliver of distrust Corey carried around made him want to protect the *final frontier*. He still felt vulnerable when it came to his body. Sharing that kind of physical intimacy with James—he wasn't sure he was ready.

The plan was to drop James off at his hotel downtown, then cab home, have dinner, and grab a shower. They'd meet up again around nine that evening and head to the Pride Dance event happening in a downtown nightclub. He'd be meeting

James outside his hotel.

"So, this dance tonight … do lots of people go?" James asked.

"It'll be packed."

"All locals?"

"No, people come from all over. You were lucky to get a hotel room."

"I'm a bit nervous."

Corey nudged James' shoulder. "About all the gay people?"

"No. About meeting your friends. What if they don't like me?"

"Doesn't matter. I love you. That's all that matters."

The dramatic swoon James tossed Corey's way was all he needed to see. James was as deeply in love with him as he was with James. No words needed to be spoken.

Twenty minutes later, they pulled up outside James' hotel. It was going to be hard to let James out of his sight. He reached over and clutched James' hand.

"I'll see you soon," Corey said.

"You won't be able to get rid of me."

James kissed him, a passionate kiss full of longing. Then jumped out of the cab. James took the stairs into the hotel. Corey wanted to chase after him. Before he could give it a second thought, the cab pulled away from the curb. The separation churned up his stomach.

Nine o'clock wouldn't come soon enough.

The ride to Black Mountain and Corey's apartment was quiet. After such an emotional reunion, the silence was heart-wrenching. He could have easily followed James into his hotel room, been consumed by his lips, been caressed by his hands— been made love to. His desire to be ravished by James was strong. He had to be stronger.

Walking into his apartment, only Gus came to greet him. Syd just looked up at him from his place on the sofa. "You having a lazy day, Syd?" He encouraged Syd off the sofa and hooked them both up with their leashes. A quick trip outside was all they needed. They'd had a long walk before he'd gone to the airport to pick up James. Syd hadn't been impressed with the exertion required.

Corey ruffled their furry heads once they were back inside.

Both dogs settled on the sofa as he opened the fridge. He was making burgers tonight. He'd bought a barbeque last week and had cooked on it every night since. He pulled out a bag of lettuce. Some for the burgers. Some for a salad. It would only take him thirty minutes or so to whip everything up. The burger patties were already made. He'd formed a stack of them earlier in the day. Corey smiled. It was something he and James shared, a love for cooking.

He was sad James couldn't join him. They'd had so much fun cooking curry together when they'd first started hanging out. That weekend snowboarding up at Big White. The weekend everything had changed for them. The weekend they had blown the doors off their relationship being a simple friendship. It had been a short hop from that to love—for both of them.

Having James at his apartment was out of the question, though. Way too much temptation. They would go to this dance together tonight. Tomorrow was Drag Brunch, then the Festival in the Park. That would leave them Sunday night to be together. If he was feeling it.

Corey opened two cans of dog food. Feeding the dogs first meant they would be less likely to beg for scraps from him. He was a pushover when it came to his boys. They knew it and they exploited it. People food was out of the question, though.

He knew better than to do that.

They both jumped off the sofa and Gus barely breathed as he chomped and swallowed his whole can of food. Syd was a bit fussier, only finishing half of it. When he wandered off, Gus finished the leftovers. That was followed by a slurp of water; most of it landing on the floor.

Corey arranged everything on the counter for his dinner, stepped outside, and fired up the grill. Before long, he was seated on a rickety, old chair on his patio digging into delicious burgers and salad. The patio was cool. Protected from the sun. He cracked open a beer.

He mulled over what he was wearing tonight. He was going to gay it up a bit. He had some silver bootie shorts and a pink mesh top he was dying to have James see him in. They had discussed it. He didn't want James to feel uncomfortable being seen with him, but James had expressed excitement about seeing Corey in something sexy and revealing. Some very lude language had ensued. After that phone call, Corey knew exactly what James wanted to do to him once he had his hands on him again. Remembering that conversation—*fuck*—his cock hardened at the thought.

He finished the beer and rose from the chair. He needed a shower. The day had been sweaty and uncomfortable. *And then there was that shower*. Corey groaned. Damned if that wasn't a memory worth repeating. James' mouth and tongue all over his body. So tentative but hungry.

Corey opened the door to his apartment.

Not now, Corey.

He turned on the shower. He hoped James had settled into his hotel room all right. He was looking forward to tonight. He was finally going to be able to introduce James to his friends. Friends that included his exes. It was a small town. You had to be flexible that way.

Corey soaped up his hair.

He'd been talking his friends' ears off about James. How they knew each other. How they'd bumped into each other. The weekend snowboarding, the cooking—the kiss—the sex. His gay friends had wanted all the details about their bedroom and shower encounters. His straight guy friends—not so much. Corey grinned. The groans, fake vomiting, and ear plugging that ensued had been hilarious. They were fun to torture. A few of them were coming to the dance tonight.

Corey stepped out of the shower and messed up the curls on his head. They would fall naturally the way he wanted them. A bit of product would hold them. He'd had his undercut shaved almost down to the skin the day before so it would be fresh for James.

He was nervous. Nervous for James to meet his friends. Nervous to see what Sunday night might hold for them. Nervous about whether they would get their easy intimacy back.

He checked his phone. It was already eight-thirty. Dinner had been late. James' flight had come in at six-fifteen. He would need to take the dogs out one more time before he took off. He called up an app for a local cab company and put in his request for pickup. There was no way he was going to drive tonight. Cocktails were in order. Lots of them.

Dogs dealt with, Corey tucked his phone into his shorts and climbed into the cab.

James was waiting for him outside the hotel. Corey was on time. There had been a moment when he thought he might not be. Emerging from his apartment in his revealing outfit, Corey thought the cab driver might take off without him. He had certainly given him some dirty looks.

"Wow." James took a few steps back, his gaze wandering up and down Corey's body. The silver shorts were skintight; the pink mesh top highlighted his tanned pecs. "That is some outfit." He wandered back toward Corey, wrapped his arms around him, and buried his face against Corey's neck. "You have no idea how much I want to strip it off you," he whispered.

Corey snorted, laughing. "Oh ... pretty sure I can guess."

James let go with some reluctance. "Where are we headed?"

"Just a few blocks from here. We won't have to line up. I know the doorman."

"Lead the way."

James held back as Corey walked away. Corey could feel James' eyes on his ass. James caught up and slung his arm around Corey's shoulders. It felt good to walk the streets like that.

They weren't the only ones.

The community was *out* in the city tonight.

Out and proud.

Chapter Twenty-Three | James

Taking his eyes off Corey's ass in those shorts had taken a significant amount of effort. Corey's ass was tight and high. His thighs—toned, solid, formed by years of snowboarding. And the shirt—it permitted James glimpses of a chest he had kissed and tasted every square inch of.

James hauled himself away from staring and jogged to catch up to Corey. He put his arm around Corey's shoulders. They were together. He wanted everyone to know that. James hummed with satisfaction as Corey put his arm around his waist and hooked his thumb beneath the wide band of James' shorts. He wasn't sure what to call what they had. They hadn't had the *boyfriend* talk yet. It seemed unnecessary. They were in love with each other. Surely, being boyfriends was implied. For some reason, he was scared to bring it up.

He could hear the music before they reached the corner situated a block away from the nightclub. The lineup outside was long—and colorful. Corey was by far the hottest guy there in his opinion, but some of the outfits in the line were serious contenders.

"Come on." Corey hauled on his arm and pulled James toward the door. Corey was right. They didn't have to wait in line. They walked directly from warm, night breezes into an onslaught of thumping chaos. James could feel it in his chest. There were bodies everywhere. Standing in lines for drinks, huddled together in groups, leaping up and down on the dance floor.

James reached for Corey's hand, found it, and clung to it. Across the room, an eclectic collection of people leaped to their feet and waved frantically in their direction. They were occupying one of the few tables scattered around the place.

Corey waved back and pulled James toward them.

He could feel the eyes on him. Judging—measuring. Was he hot? Did he look friendly? Was he good enough for Corey? He'd be under scrutiny for the entire night. Scrutiny he was willing to endure. He wanted Corey's friends to like him—to tell Corey he'd found a good guy.

Introductions were made but James was too nervous to remember any of their names. Some he hadn't even heard; the music was so loud. Three of the guys were dressed like Corey. Two were not. Those two looked like jocks thrust into an unplanned night out. One person was dressed to look like an anime character. Guy or girl, he wasn't sure. The final two, James decided to refer to them as *they* for the moment. He'd have to ask them their pronouns when he got a chance.

James slipped into the booth beside Corey. Corey leaned toward him. "Can I get you a drink?"

"More than one, please."

"I'll load us up." Corey reached across the table and grabbed the arm of a very attractive dark-haired guy. He looked up and smiled at Corey. It made James feel uneasy.

James scowled. He wasn't sure where that feeling had come from. A crazy bubbling. Corey jerked his chin in the direction of the bar and the guy nodded his head in agreement.

Corey took off across the dance floor with the guy—Todd. James remembered his name now. It might even be the same Todd that Corey worked with.

"Those two don't change," someone shouted in James' ear. *What the hell did that mean?*

James turned to look at the guy talking to him. "What?"

"The party boys." The guy nudged James. "They used to see each other."

James looked across the dance floor toward the bar. Corey and Todd were laughing, shoving, and hanging off each other as they waited for their drink orders. James crossed his arms.

Corey hadn't mentioned that one of his exes was going to be there. That he worked with his exe. That he was still friends with his exe. The two men pranced back across the floor together.

James eyed the drinks Corey set down in front of him. Then looked up at Todd. Heat crept up his back. He closed his eyes and willed the emotion overtaking him to dissipate. Jealousy had never been something he'd encountered before. He grunted. No, that wasn't true. When that guy had been hitting on Corey up at Big White, he'd felt a wave of it. He needed to let it go.

Corey cuddled up against James and kissed his cheek.

"Wanna dance with me?"

"Do I get to hold you?"

"As tight and hot as you want."

James smirked. "That's what he said."

Corey positively shrieked and threw his arms around James' neck. He ran his hands into James' hair and descended on his lips. The kiss was hot and desperate. Fueled by the low lighting and thunderous music. Corey slipped his tongue into James' mouth, teasing—tasting. His mewls and moans vibrated in James' throat. The fact they were in public melted away. This was a safe space.

Corey relaxed his hold, sucked on James' bottom lip, then released it.

"Yum," he said in James' ear.

All the jealousy James had been feeling disappeared. Corey had just made a very public announcement that he and James were together. That they were a couple.

Corey pulled him onto the dance floor. It wasn't one of his strengths—dancing. But James suspected Corey wouldn't care. Corey, on the other hand, was an incredible dancer. His lean, muscular body kept fluid time with each beat. Corey turned and backed up against James. Corey's back to James' chest. James wrapped his arms around Corey's waist, moving to the music as Corey's ass, hips swaying, put pressure on James' cock. It had already been paying attention.

"You are so hot," James growled in Corey's ear.

Corey spun out of his arms, grinning, and winked at him.

The rest of the night, they barely left the dance floor. Quick dashes to fill up on cocktails. Bathroom breaks—and back to dancing. James was exhausted by the time it seemed the dance party was winding down. Corey glistened; he'd been sweating so much.

Corey had his phone out as they headed for the door. His friends followed, stumbling along, hollering, and hanging onto each other. There had been more than a few drinking challenges.

Corey wasn't in much better shape than his friends. James was doing his best to keep Corey on his feet. Unsuccessfully. His own were opting to deceive him.

He was lucky he didn't have far to walk back to the hotel.

Corey hammered on his phone screen with his index finger. "Stupid cab app." Distracted by his phone, Corey nearly landed in the street after tripping off the curb. James caught him.

"Whoops." Corey giggled.

Todd hailed a passing cab and lurched toward it. He flung the back door open.

"Corey … Corey … come on … cab."

"Nah." Corey shook his head. "Changed mind. Wanna stay with James."

Todd stumbled on the edge of a storm grate. "Corey … come on. Share the cab."

Corey furrowed his brow and looked at James. "I should … I should go."

James pulled on Corey's hand.

"Wait … why?"

"Tomorrow, James … tomorrow. Too drunk."

Corey slipped out of James' grasp and careened toward the cab. He blew James a kiss, then fell headlong into the backseat.

The snide, calculated look Todd gave James before he climbed into the cab with Corey; like he had successfully kidnapped Corey from him, had James reaching for the car door handle just as the cab pulled away. It sped off into the distance.

Fuck.

James nearly pitched his phone at the ground. There was that jealousy again. Jealousy and anger. Corey had effectively been taken from him. Who knew what Todd had planned. Corey was drunk, unable to defend himself. James clenched his fists tight, his entire body prickling with heat.

The things he wanted to do to that guy—Todd, if he touched Corey.

He looked up and down the street. He had Corey's home address on his phone. He was nearly knocked down by a car as he leaped out and hailed a cab. When he arrived at Corey's apartment, he wasn't there. One of the dogs barked at him through the door when he knocked, but no Corey.

There were no lights on. The place was empty.

James sunk into an old chair on Corey's patio. It was

another fifteen minutes before a cab pulled up at the end of the driveway and Corey spilled out. He had a stern look on his face.

Finally.

James launched himself toward Corey's door as Corey stumbled down the driveway. Corey almost took a few spills. Dropped his phone twice. At the door, he collided with James.

"Whatcha doin' here?" Corey fidgeted with his lock until it turned for him.

"What do you think? That guy yanked you away from me."

"Todd?" Corey shook his head. "No … I wanted to go home. Don't want to have sex with you." He pouted as he looked at James and nearly lost his balance. "Asshole kissed me."

"What?" James gripped Corey's arm. His face flushed red; heat burned the back of his neck. He knew Todd had been up to something.

Corey yanked his arm away. "Stop. You're hurting me."

James could feel his anger rising. He wasn't sure who he was mad at more. Todd for taking advantage. Or Corey for allowing himself to be put in that position. Surely, Corey must have known how Todd felt about him. He worked with him practically every day.

"Did you kiss him back?"

Corey shoved him. "Fuck off, James! Course not!" He opened his door, stepped in, turned around, and gave James another shove. He pressed his hand to James' chest. "You are *not* coming in with me. You're as much an asshole as he is. Leave." He slammed the door and locked it.

James ran his hands into his hair.

Panic.

Absolute fucking panic.

James hammered on the door. "Corey, I'm sorry. I didn't mean it."

"Asshole! Leave!" Corey shouted through the door.

James wanted to pound on the door some more, but he knew it would be pointless. He'd screwed up. How could he think Corey would betray him by kissing someone else?

"Fuck!"

He slammed the heel of his hand into the siding of the house and placed his forehead against the smooth surface. That was it. He'd fucked up and broken any trust he had built with Corey.

It was over.

Things had been going so well. He scrubbed his hands into his hair. Corey had every right to dump him. He'd let his jealousy overtake him. Corey was right.

He couldn't be trusted with Corey's heart.

As James trudged up the driveway, the door flew open. Corey was wide-eyed and looked terrified. He ran up the driveway and grabbed James' arm. "Something's wrong with Syd!"

"What? What do you mean?"

Corey hauled him down the driveway and into the apartment. "James ... please."

"Where is he?"

"The bedroom. He's lying on the floor. He won't move and there's vomit all over the apartment." Corey led the way to his bedroom.

James kneeled beside Syd and checked his eyes and gums. He didn't look good at all. "Has been eating normally? Drinking water."

"No." Corey stroked Syd's head. "He's been off his food since yesterday. I figured he was drinking water while I was at work. But maybe he wasn't."

"What about when you take him out? Has he been doing his business? Aside from peeing."

Corey shook his head. "No, but I didn't think anything of it."

James touched Syd's stomach. "His belly is swollen, and he's dehydrated." He exhaled. "It might be a twisted bowel. It sometimes happens in bigger dogs."

Corey gripped James' arm. "What do we do?"

"Does Kelowna have an animal emergency hospital?"

"One."

"Call them. Tell them that you have a vet tech with you, and he suspects a twisted bowel."

"Right … okay." Corey rose to his feet and fished his phone out of his shorts. It took him a few seconds to find the number. He waited impatiently for someone to pick up. When they did, he relayed the information. He looked at James. "They want us to bring him in right away."

It's the response James had expected. This was an emergency. They needed to get Syd there as soon as possible. Load him into Corey's car and drive like hell.

Except, they were both too drunk to drive.

"Call your sister," James said. "We're going to need a ride."

"We'll be right there." Corey ended the call with the hospital and contacted his sister. "Syd is sick. I need to take him to Emergency. James and I can't drive. We've been out drinking." He nodded his head, listening to his sister. He disconnected the call. "She'll be right here."

James ran his hand down Syd's side. He was breathing heavily. Slow labored breaths. He looked at Corey. He didn't have the heart to tell him Syd might not make it.

Ten minutes later, Kala burst in through the front door.

"Where is Syd? What happened?"

Corey left the bedroom. "James thinks it's a twisted bowel."

Kala looked at James and furrowed her brow. James decided to ignore her. He hoisted Syd into his arms and walked past Kala. "Let's get him into your car." There were more important things to worry about than Kala's disapproval of him being there.

"I'm going in the back with him," Corey said. James settled Syd on the backseat of the car and Corey climbed in beside him. Corey set Syd's head on his lap, trembling as he stroked Syd's fur.

James climbed into the passenger seat. There was a moment when Kala just stared at him then she started the car. The trip took longer than James felt comfortable with. Syd needed IV fluids fast to improve his condition so he was suitable for surgery.

He turned in his seat and caught Corey's attention.

"He's going to be all right," James said.

He offered his hand. Corey clung to it like a life preserver. It seemed, for now, Corey's anger and ill feelings toward James were on hold. They needed to concentrate on Syd.

At the animal hospital, Corey carried Syd into an exam room. All three of them crowded into the small space. It was almost three in the morning. The veterinarian didn't look impressed, but he was professional in his approach. Corey's revealing outfit did receive a strange look, though.

James relayed what had happened to the vet. Corey draped his body over Syd, kissing and rubbing his head. "Come on." James pulled Corey away so the vet could do his work.

The vet checked Syd's color and palpated his stomach. "We'll take an x-ray then get him on some fluids. There's not much we can do until the morning when the rest of the staff is in and he's well enough to undergo surgery if it's needed. Go home. We'll stay in contact."

"Is he going to be all right?" Corey stroked Syd's head as James rubbed circles in the center of Corey's back. He wished he could take Corey's pain away.

"We'll know more once we get the radiographs back," the vet said.

Corey turned and hugged James as the vet took Syd from the exam room, through the door, and into the back. "I can't lose him." He looked at James. "Tell me I won't lose him."

James simply held him. "I can't tell you that. I want to … but I can't."

Kala touched Corey's arm. "Let's get you home."

There was silence once they closed the car doors. Kala turned to face James who was again sitting in the passenger seat. "Which hotel are you at? I'll drop you off."

Corey lurched forward and grabbed Kala's shoulder. "No. He's coming home with me."

A long breath escaped James' chest.

Oh, thank God.

A feeling of elation filled his heart. He had thought it was over between them. Corey had shoved him and called him an asshole. To him, that sounded like he'd messed things up for good.

James reached for Corey's hand. Again, Corey clung to it. The tingling sensation was mixed with intense sorrow. James remembered when he lost Patches. Corey had to be going through hell.

"Corey." Kala turned her attention to him. "Are you sure you want to do that?"

"I need him, Kala. He's my boyfriend and I need him with me tonight."

Boyfriend.

There it was. James hadn't been sure. He'd settled on lovers. Being boyfriends meant Corey was open to the idea of their relationship becoming more serious. He squeezed Corey's hand. *It already was.* They were in love with each other, but that didn't necessarily mean Corey wanted to spend his life with him. This was confirmation that Corey wasn't abandoning what they'd been building back together. All was not lost. He still had a chance to earn Corey's trust back.

"Okay." Kala pulled out of the parking lot. It wasn't until they arrived in Corey's driveway that Corey let go of James' hand.

Once inside, Corey poured them each a glass of water, accompanied by a couple of aspirin. The crisis had sobered them up somewhat, but they were still in for a lot of suffering.

Corey wandered into the bedroom and stripped off his clothes. James could see Corey's nude silhouette through his open door. He sighed, opened the linen closet door, found a blanket and pillow, and headed for the sofa. He managed to arrange a bed for himself.

James did his best not to peek when Corey headed into the bathroom. Exhausted, he snuggled into the light blanket and was almost asleep when Corey approached the back of the sofa.

"James, what are you doing out here?"

James looked up at Corey. "I'm an asshole, remember. You told me to leave. I didn't think you'd want me in bed with you."

"Oh, for god's sake." Corey wandered into his bedroom, slipped into bed, and tossed open the bedding on the opposite side of him. "I was mad at you for thinking I would consider kissing anyone else. I wasn't ditching you."

James made his way over to the doorway of the bedroom. "I didn't believe it when I said it. It just slipped out."

Corey smiled. "That's what he said."

James shook his head, laughing softly. "You're sure you want me in there with you."

"Please get in." Corey patted the bed. "I need you with me tonight."

James stripped his t-shirt off over his head. He pulled his shorts off. Left his underwear on even though Corey was naked. He didn't want to make any assumptions, especially because Corey's dog was in critical condition. Corey just needed some comfort from him, not sex.

He was soon proven wrong.

"I want you to make love to me," Corey said. "Make me forget for a few minutes."

James turned to face Corey and nuzzled Corey's ear with his nose. "You sure?"

"Positive. Why do you think I was in the bathroom for so long."

"I mean are you sure you're ready? This is a big deal."

"James … I love you. That's all that matters."

"I want you to be sure."

"James, you're the first thing I think of in the morning—the last thing at night. All day long. You occupy my every thought. I need to feel your love. I need that intimacy back."

James kissed Corey's cheek. "Then I'm with you all the way. I'm yours."

Corey flipped over onto his stomach and pulled open his beside dresser drawer. He grabbed a condom and some lube and dumped it all on his pillow. James lifted the condom and ripped it open with his teeth. He placed the open packet back on Corey's pillow. His cock wasn't hard enough to put it on yet. He had other plans anyway.

"Stay on your stomach," he said to Corey.

"Why? What are you up to?"

James scurried down the bed and encouraged Corey to open his legs. Corey looked back at James as he lay on his stomach between Corey's legs.

"Fuck, James … are you sure?"

"I've been doing research."

"Are you telling me the good little church boy has been watching gay porn?"

"Some of that time I spent on my knees in Pastor Jim's office, I was thinking about what I had seen in those videos." He smiled and kissed Corey's ass cheek. "Bit of a struggle not to get hard."

"My tiger is such a bad boy."

James grinned. He loved when Corey called him that. Tiger. He let out a roar that sent Corey into a fit of giggles. This was the ease between them they had been missing.

Corey bit his bottom lip as James parted Corey's cheeks and ventured between them. He used his thumbs to expose his target. He darted his tongue out testing the feel and taste of Corey's hole. He was musky—sweaty from dancing earlier. James buried his face deeper.

"Oh, fuck … right there." Corey gripped the pillow, tipped his head forward, and splayed his legs wider. James tickled and licked, circling Corey's warm hole. It was heaven being this close to him again. Tasting his body—making him squirm and sigh.

James tried to press the tip of his tongue past the ring. It wasn't letting him in. He used his thumbs to pry it open, then dove at it again.

Corey tipped his hips up, whispering, "Fuck … fuck … fuck," under his breath. After four more assaults, Corey reached back and swatted James' head. "Enough. I need you inside me."

James came up for air and kissed Corey's tailbone. "Hand me everything."

Corey handed James the condom and lube after James stripped his underwear off. This time James didn't need instruction on how to prepare himself and Corey. He'd been practicing. James gripped Corey's hip with one hand, his cock with the other. The whole scene was almost too much, being back with Corey like this.

James nearly wept as he pushed his cock past the ring of Corey's hole. Corey wouldn't have exposed his heart and shared his body like this unless some level of trust had been restored.

He placed his hands on either side of Corey's body and sunk his cock deep. Corey groaned and shifted forward. It was heavenly—and good. So incredibly good and pure.

He loved this man more than life.

James leaned forward and kissed the back of Corey's neck then lowered his weight on him. His chest plastered to Corey's back, he hooked his arms beneath Corey's shoulders so he could whisper in his ear. "I love you so much."

Corey mewled and sighed as James shifted. "I love you too."

James undulated his hips; slid out then back in. Then again—and again. The intimacy of the act stirred something in him. Love flowed rampant through his veins.

This was the man he wanted to spend the rest of his life with.

He needed to see his face.

James withdrew and encouraged Corey to roll onto his back. He covered Corey's mouth with his, kissing him with an ardency they had never experienced before. Corey wrapped his legs around James's waist and rolled his hips up so their hard cocks slipped past each other.

"Please, James."

James responded to Corey's desire and slipped back into Corey's body. He kept his rhythm steady and smooth, unlike the first time Corey had trusted him enough to seek out this level of intimacy from him. Corey gripped James' forearms, his nails digging in.

Corey closed his eyes and licked his lips.

"Yes … please, yes."

James looked down at Corey. He appeared serene and at peace.

Angelic.

Absolutely angelic.

"I want to see your eyes." James brushed his thumb across Corey's lips. "Then I want to kiss you again. And I never want to stop kissing you."

Corey smiled and opened his eyes. The love staring up at him was heart-stopping. "We'll have to come up for air sometimes."

"I don't need air. I only need you." James thrust his cock high until Corey groaned and clung tighter to him. He increased his pace. Corey moved his hands to James' shoulders and dug in hard with his fingers. He hauled James back to his mouth.

Flat out on Corey's body, his weight on Corey like the first day they had hung out together—it brought back so many memories. James crested. The rhythm of their bodies as they moved as one had pushed him over the edge. He was right. There was purity in this.

Pure unconditional love.

James relaxed for a moment then slid down Corey's body

to take Corey's cock into his mouth. Pre-cum covered the tip. He started there first then pulled Corey's foreskin tight to his body. He descended on his shaft. Corey tipped his hips up and combed his fingers through James' hair, keeping pressure on James's head.

The demanding nature of the move thrilled James into bobbing faster.

"Oh, fuck." Corey clutched a clump of James' hair. "That's it." He grunted and his cock hit the back of James' throat and spilled free. James accepted it all, then slipped off Corey's cock.

"Come back to me," Corey whispered.

James crawled up the bed. Corey cupped James' face and kissed him. His tongue darted in, tasting everything and challenging James for dominance. James relaxed, allowing Corey to take what he wanted from him. James would give him anything if he asked—anything.

Corey released his mouth.

"I'll never betray you again," James said as he touched Corey's lips.

"I know. I believe you." Corey sighed. "I've forgiven you."

James' eyes burned as he looked at Corey. Tears welled up. He'd been absolved by the most incredible man. Staring into Corey's eyes, James knew he would be Corey's forever.

Chapter Twenty-Four | Corey

Corey hadn't intended to give himself to James tonight. But after the emergency with Syd, he realized life and time were too precious to waste. He was in love with the man who had carried his dog so tenderly, carefully put him in the back seat of the car, and held his hand in the car.

James had stood there in the exam room with him, stroking Syd's fur, telling the veterinarian what he had observed. Corey had been too overwrought to speak. The affection James had shown Syd; a dog he had only just met, melted Corey's heart. Syd was an extension of him. James knew that. The last sliver of trust had kicked back into place.

And forgiveness. So much forgiveness.

After that. He had needed James.

The connection—the intimacy.

Corey grinned as he stared up at the ceiling.

And the sex … James had been both adorable and hot as he pursued what he wanted.

"What are you thinking about?" James asked then kissed Corey's nose.

"You. Always you." Corey trailed the back of his fingers down James' arm. He winked at James. "Everything live up to expectations after watching all that porn?"

"Better." James rose on one arm, leaned over, and kissed Corey.

The ringer on Corey's phone broke the moment.

Corey pushed James aside and jerked up off the mattress.

He nearly knocked his phone off the bedside table in his haste to answer it.

"It's the vet," he said to James. He answered the call. He nearly cried. It was good news. He felt like he could breathe again. Syd was responding well to fluids. The x-ray verified it was something happening in his bowels. Likely not a twist. They'd know more once they opened him up. The surgery was scheduled for seven in the morning.

"We'll call you when he comes out of surgery," the vet said then hung up.

James moved closer to Corey and held his shoulder. "Is everything all right?"

"He's responding well to the fluids." Corey tucked his back against James' chest and hauled the thin sheet over them. "Might not be a twist. They're going to operate at seven."

"We should know something by nine if all goes well." James rolled off the bed and headed for the bathroom. After washing his hands, he returned to his place beside Corey.

Corey felt a lot calmer when James draped an arm over his body, hugged him, and kissed the back of his head.

"Try to sleep," James whispered.

Corey wasn't sure sleep would find him. Syd was on his mind. The pain he must be in. How scared he must be without his brother. Confused by why he was in a strange place.

Guilt.

He felt so much guilt.

"I should have known he was sick sooner."

"Don't do that to yourself. Dogs get sick all the time from eating stuff they shouldn't. You had no way of knowing it was something serious."

"I let him down."

"Corey, you rushed him to the vet as soon as you realized

something was wrong. There's nothing else you could have done."

"How come it feels like I could have?"

"Because you love him."

Corey lifted James' hand and kissed it. "I'm glad you were here."

"I want to be here for you … for everything."

What?

"What do you mean?" Corey wrinkled his brow. What was James getting at? Now that they'd had sex, James seemed to be moving fast.

James kissed the back of Corey's neck. "I want to go to bed with you like this … every night."

Every night.

Corey rolled over to face James. "You want us to live together?" James stroked his hand up and down Corey's arm. James was trembling. This must be terrifying for him.

"I do," James answered.

The sequence of those two words gave Corey shivers. Marriage wasn't on the table. Living together hadn't even been on Corey's mind. He'd only just decided to trust James again. Could he take it one step further and fully commit to this man? Make a change like moving in with him?

"Where would we live?" Corey asked.

"I don't know." James licked his lips. "Here?"

"You have a proper career and your animal shelter. I couldn't ask you to leave all that."

"You have your sister and your parents."

Corey shrugged. "They could visit."

"My apartment is small."

"As small as this one?"

"No, but we should probably rent a house. Give the dogs

somewhere to run."

"The dogs and one very old cat."

James stared into Corey's eyes. "And a little garden."

"We could grow our own vegetables."

"We'd pile into bed every night with all the animals."

"I'd like that."

James studied Corey's eyes, air rushing in and out of his nose. "Are we actually doing this?"

"I think we might be." Corey pressed his lips together and then spoke. "Are you sure?"

James cupped Corey's face. "As sure as taking my next breath."

"Okay." Corey touched his forehead to James'.

"I'll move in with you," he whispered against James' lips. "Just give me time to wrap things up here. My family is going to be hesitant to support me after what you did to me. And my parents are going to want to meet you."

"Parents love me."

"These ones don't." Corey brushed his hand through James' hair. "You broke their son's heart. That's going to take a lot of convincing to prove you won't do it again."

James furrowed his brow. "I would never."

"I know that … they don't. I didn't even tell them we started seeing each other again."

"You weren't sure."

"I honestly didn't think you could change."

"But you knew how much I loved you."

Corey sighed. "You grew up in an environment of obedience. When you knelt in front of your mother and confessed that you'd sinned and I meant nothing to you, a little piece of my heart died. The fact you'd told me you were falling for me—it lost its meaning. The joy of that evaporated. I didn't believe it anymore. I thought it was all lies."

"I'm so sorry." James closed his eyes. Tears trickled down the bridge of his nose.

Corey touched James' chin, encouraging James to look at him. "You've proven that."

The glimmer of relief and love in James' eyes was stunning. Corey kissed him, the salty tears James had shed dampened Corey's lips. James' breath was hot against his mouth. He intensified the kiss, diving deep. Forgiven and trusted. They had come a long way.

Corey parted from James. "I miss what we had together. When we were in that hotel room during the Winter Games, everything was fresh and new."

"I took that away."

"But in some twisted way, it brought us closer together. I never stopped loving you. When I saw you at that bar, my heart cried out, yearning for you, urging me on like it was going to refuse to beat again if I didn't run after you. It knew that you were *my* forever."

"And you're mine."

"James, I was so scared you'd turn me away."

"I was terrified. Seeing you—I knew I wanted you back. Nothing else mattered. The church—my parents—nothing. Hearing you wanted to take things slow—hurt. But I understood. I didn't deserve to have you back in my life. You took a chance on me."

"I'm glad I did." Corey cupped James' face and kissed him. The love he had for this man was boundless. He had listened to his heart—and it had led him to where he needed to be.

In James' arms.

He deepened the kiss, then hesitated.

Syd.

Corey ended the kiss and rolled onto his back. He retrieved his phone from the bedside table and lay it on his chest. "I need to close my eyes for a few minutes."

James lay his hand on Corey's hip, his arm draped across Corey's stomach. He rolled in against Corey and kissed his shoulder. "Syd will be coming with us to Victoria. I can feel it."

"Yes. That's the image I'm running through my mind. Us in a nice house. The dogs racing around in the backyard. Us cooking in *our* kitchen."

"I love that daydream."

"And I love you," Corey whispered.

"Love you too. Now sleep."

Corey could feel his consciousness slipping. Syd was in good hands. James was at his side. They were moving in together. Their love was growing.

He blinked a few times, then drifted off to sleep.

The jarring sound of the phone ringing made Corey jump. He lifted it from his chest and looked at the screen. It was the vet. He nudged James to wake him up.

"Hello." Corey was cautious as he answered the call. He didn't want to get his hopes up. Plus, his head was groggy from a hangover. He wasn't sure how much information he could process.

James rose on one elbow and scrubbed a hand across his face. It seemed they were both feeling a bit rough. Corey put the call on speakerphone so James could hear.

"We opened him up. Good news. It was just an obstruction."

Corey closed his eyes, praising whatever deity had been watching over his dog.

"What was it?" James asked.

"A sock. More common than we'd like to see."

"You got it out?" Corey asked.

"Removed it and stitched up his bowel. He'll heal up nicely."

"When can he come home?" Corey asked as he made a mental note to keep all socks off the floor from now on. They did not need a repeat of this.

"We'll keep him for a day. Make sure he's eating and passing stool all right."

Corey held the phone closer to his mouth. "Can I come to visit?"

"Sure. We're open until six. You can come anytime."

"Thank you," the men said in unison, then Corey ended the call.

"A sock." Corey tossed his phone onto the covers. "What the hell?"

"You'd be amazed what dogs swallow. Bits of tennis balls. Lego. I've even seen a whole obstruction of G-strings. Dogs are weird."

"And this cat of yours is better?"

James smiled. "Well … okay, she throws up the occasional hairball. Is obsessed with her own tail. And is completely inaccurate when she uses the litter box."

"No swallowing socks, though."

"Nope."

Corey rolled to face James. "I need you again."

"Like need me … need me?"

"I want you towering above me, gentle, looking into my eyes, kissing me—making love to me. With everything that is happening, I need the comfort of your touch. When I'm with you like that—intimate … I feel like the world can't hurt me.

That I'm protected."

James brushed his knuckles down Corey's cheek.

"And safe. I feel the same way."

Corey sighed as James took his mouth. This was the man he was going to spend the rest of his life with. He could feel it in his bones. Their time together would always be precious.

Their life together would be long and full.

Without question.

His heart truly trusted James with his life.

Chapter Twenty-Five | James

James stood at the bottom of the slope behind the orange fencing. His heart was in his throat. Corey's final run was next. It was his last competition of the day. He'd scored well so far despite being away for a year. James had done well too. He and Corey had almost tied in Big Air.

Corey had won by a slim margin.

They'd been training hard. Heading to Calgary to regain their skills. There had been some flak from some of the other competitors when the news broke that he and Corey were a couple, but they'd ignored it. Their love of the sport overshadowed everything.

The interview requests had filtered in from the sports news agencies. Mainly because they were back competing, but it seemed some people wanted to hear about two snowboarding greats who had found gay love with each other.

Corey skittered to a stop by the fence near James and turned to watch the scoreboard. Within moments, top scores lit up the board. James grabbed Corey over the fence and pulled him into his arms. Corey had won first place in both of his events today. Proud didn't cover it.

"You did it!" James gripped Corey's face and kissed his cheek. "You're back, baby."

Corey, rolling through full-on laughter, pounded James on the back. Corey was breathless from exertion. His laugh was ragged and heaving.

"Go ... go." James shoved Corey. He'd been called to the

podium. Another first-place medal to decorate their home. A home they had made together.

Three weeks after deciding to move in together, and after James had spent considerable effort convincing Corey's parents that he would never hurt their son again, Corey had packed up his dogs and his belongings and moved to Victoria. They'd struggled for space in the apartment until they found a house for rent out in Metchosin. A three-bedroom house with lots of space. It was far from downtown, but it was on five acres. They'd made it their own.

Syd and Gus had the run of the place. Florence preferred the deck. After much debate, they'd picked up a miniature horse and a pot-bellied pig to add to their menagerie. They'd been lucky. Kala had decided to follow them, needing a change. Her house and pet-sitting services were essential for them to be able to compete and train … and work. Their schedule was busy.

James had retained his job at the veterinary clinic and his volunteer position at the animal shelter. Corey had joined him at the shelter. He loved the interaction with the animals. It had been a struggle to keep Corey from adopting any more of them. Corey had picked up another job in a sporting goods store, but the plan was that once he finished competing for good, he was going to go back to school and become a veterinary technician himself.

They lived their lives in tandem. Two pieces of a two-piece puzzle—bonded to each other forever. And then some. Recently, there had been talk about marriage and children.

Corey held up the medal over his head. James' heart swelled with love for him.

His one and only.

The man that had captured his heart from the first time he'd smiled at him.

His Corey.

The love of his life.

Dear Reader

I hope you enjoyed reading *Snowblind.*

Please take a moment to review this book on the website of the store where you purchased your copy of *Snowblind.*

If you would like to touch base and say hello to the author, you can email them at: leigh@leighjarrett.com

About the Author

Leigh Jarrett (she/he) is an unabashedly queer, quirky, and passionate author of Contemporary MM+ Romantic Fiction. Their published contemporary works include warm and always sexy HEA romances as well as dark romances filled with grit, trauma, and angst.

In their hometown of Victoria, BC, Canada, Leigh can be found nestled up with their fabulously supportive wife and trusty laptop or enjoying the wondrous Vancouver Island outdoors.

Please consider subscribing to Leigh's newsletter to stay up to date with their new releases and promos. If you're interested in MM+ Fantasy and Paranormal Romance, check out one of Leigh's other pen names, JT Fader, on their JT Fader Fantasticals website and newsletter jtfader.com.

To connect with Leigh Jarrett:

Email: leigh@leighjarrett.com

Website and newsletter: leighjarrett.com

You can also find Leigh on Bluesky

Other Books by Leigh Jarrett

"Find love in the least expected place."
An Enemies to Lovers M/M Gay Romance

Merlot Rebellion

"Risking it all to follow your heart."
A Found Family M/M Bisexual Romance

Capital Adoration

"Brave enough to pursue love."
An Age Gap M/M Gay Romance

Pacific Pursuit

"Learning a new path to love."
A Roommates to Lovers Bisexual Awakening M/M Romance

Academic Adoration

"Recovering true love."
A Second Chance Hurt/Comfort M/M Romance

Drag Undivided

"Strumming your way to love."
A Grumpy/Sunshine Gay Awakening M/M Romance

Rhythmic Bliss